MISS CLARE REMEMBERS

MISS CLARE
REMEMBERS

by "Miss Read"

Illustrated by J. S. Goodall

Houghton Mifflin Company Boston
The Riverside Press Cambridge
1963

First American Edition 1963
Copyright © 1962 by "Miss Read"
All rights reserved including the right to
reproduce this book or parts thereof in any form
Library of Congress Catalog Card Number: 63-11194

THE RIVERSIDE PRESS, *Cambridge, Massachusetts*
Printed in the U.S.A.

*To
My Father
with love*

He who, in the vale of obscurity, can brave adversity, can behave with tranquillity and indifference, is truly great.

OLIVER GOLDSMITH

The Disabled Soldier

PART ONE *Caxley*

CHAPTER I

A FINGER of sunlight, wavering across the white counterpane, woke Miss Clare from a light sleep.

The old lady lay for a while, without moving, watching it tremble like water across the bed and down the uneven bulging wall of her cottage bedroom.

She knew the time without troubling to turn her head to consult the china clock which ticked busily on her bedside table. Her own easy waking, and the strength and direction of the sunbeam, told her that it was a little before six o'clock on this June morning.

And there was no need to get up, thought Miss Clare, with a little shock of pleasure. Each morning, since her retirement from schoolteaching, this tremor of elation had stirred her waking moments. To be freed from the tyranny of the clock, after so many years of discipline, was wholly delightful. Almost every day of her working life Dolly Clare had resolutely thrust the bedclothes from her as the clock struck six. The habit of years dies hard, and still she woke at the same time, and rose very soon after, but with the blessed relief of knowing that, at long last, her time was her own.

She lay now, frail as a bird and very still, beneath the light covers, listening to the early morning sounds. Above her a starling chattered on the chimney pot. To thwart just such nest-builders she had prudently had wire netting stretched across the mouths of the chimneys, and now she could hear the starling's

13

claws and beak plucking the wire and making metallic music. Far away a cow lowed, and farther still a train hooted imperiously as it rushed towards London. Miss Clare could have slipped back easily into slumber again.

But suddenly there came the roaring of a motor-bike kicked into life. The clock vibrated in sympathy, and Miss Clare sat upright.

'That's Jim off to work,' she said aloud. 'Time I was up.'

The motor-bike thundered by, shaking the old lady into wakefulness.

'And this is the day that Emily comes! Plenty to do today!'

She put back the bed clothes and thrust her bony legs towards a patch of warm sunlight on the rug. Miss Clare's day had begun.

It was strange, thought Miss Clare, half an hour later, moving methodically about her small kitchen, how little Emily Davis knew of the important part she had played in her own life. For almost seventy years now she and Emily had been friends. For several years they had taught side by side as pupil teachers, and when their ways had parted, weekly letters, lengthy and beautifully penned, had sustained their affection. No matter how long their partings, on meeting they fell together as sweetly as two halves of an apple. Now, in old age, the warm friendship had an added quality, for the knowledge that it must end before long quickened their love for each other.

They had first met under the steep slated roof of Beech Green school, when Emily Davis was seven years old and Dolly Clare a forlorn newcomer of six. Standing now in the kitchen, her brown breakfast egg poised in a spoon above the saucepan of bubbling water, Miss Clare looked back across the years and saw the scene as sharply as if it had all happened that morning.

*   *   *

It was the same kitchen that she and her mother had left to make their way to the nearby school. It was a wet Monday morning in March and the Clare family had moved into their new home on the Friday before. Two hours earlier Francis Clare, Dolly's father, who was a thatcher by trade, had set off to work, pushing before him a little handcart containing his tools. Upstairs lay Dolly's sister Ada, two years her senior, and smitten this morning with a timely cold and a violent cough which meant that school was out of the question for her. Envying her from the bottom of her heart, Dolly set out for the unknown, clutching her mother's hand.

'Don't you stir till I'm back, Ada,' called Mary Clare, her face tilted up to the bedroom window. 'I shan't be ten minutes.'

She hurried off so briskly that Dolly was forced to run to keep up with her. Her mother's hand was hot and comforting through the cotton glove. The child had need of comfort. New black boots pinched her toes and rubbed her heels. Her long tartan frock, decently covered with a white pinafore, bundled itself between her legs as she ran along. Her straight yellow hair had been strained to the top of her head and tied there so tightly with a black ribbon by her over-anxious mother that she could feel the skin over her temples drawn upwards in sympathy.

But her physical pain was as nothing to the ache in her heart. Fear of the ordeal before her, the entry alone into a strange and possibly hostile world was bad enough, but even this was less than the misery which had gripped her since the move from their old home at Caxley. This was the third day of grief for young Dolly Clare, the third day of mourning for her lifelong companion, her other half. Emily, her rag doll, had disappeared during the chaos of moving day, and for her young mistress the world was in ruins.

The road to the school was muddy and rutted deeply where the cart wheels made their way. This morning rain lay in long bright bands on each side of the rough flints in the centre of the lane. Other children were making their way to school, shabby satchels or plaited rush bags containing their dinner bumping on their backs. They looked curiously at breathless Dolly, scuttling at the heels of her mother, and nudged each other and whispered as they passed. Dolly was glad when they clanked over the door scraper and entered the high schoolroom.

Mr Finch, the headmaster, was a solemn figure in black with a silver watch-chain drawn across his waistcoat just on a level with Dolly's throbbing temples. The room was very quiet, and a number of children were already in their desks sitting very prim and upright, but with their eyes fixed un-

winkingly upon their new schoolfellow. Dolly was too over-
come to return their gaze, and looked at her new boots already
splashed with chalky water from the lane.

'Yes, sir, she's already been to school at Caxley,' her mother
was saying. 'She can read and reckon, and is a good hand with a
needle.'

'Date of birth?' asked Mr Finch sombrely.

'Tenth of April, sir, eighteen eighty-eight.'

'And her full name?'

'Dorothy Annie Clare, but she's called Dolly, sir.'

'I will tell my wife. She will start with her.'

'I've another girl to come. Ada, sir, she's eight, but in bed
poorly this morning.'

'Very well,' said Mr Finch with a note of dismissal in his
voice. Taking the hint, Dolly's mother gave her daughter's
cheek a swift peck and disappeared homewards, leaving her
younger child as lonely as she was ever to be.

She stood on the bare boards of the schoolroom trembling
from her tight black boots to the top knot on her head, fighting
against tears and longing for the comfort of Emily's hard
stuffed body in her arm. But Emily had gone, even as her
mother had gone, and though in an eternity of time, when the
great wall clock struck twelve, she would see her mother again,
yet Emily had gone for ever.

The figures in the desks wavered and swelled as the hot tears
pricked her eyes.

'You can sit by Emily for now,' said a woman's voice above
her head. She found herself being led to the further end of the
long room. Emily, Emily! The word beat in her head like a
bewildered bird trying to get out of a closed room. In her
present dream-like condition it seemed possible that she might
be advancing to meet her long-lost familiar again, although
the dull ache at her heart counselled otherwise.

She found herself in front of a double desk. At one side sat a grave dark child, with black hair smoothed from a centre parting to fall into two long plaits. Her eyes were grey and clear like water and her smile disclosed a gap where her two front milk teeth had gone.

'This is Emily,' said Mrs Finch.

It wasn't, of course, to Dolly Clare; but the smile was engaging and the grey eyes reassuring. And, amazingly, the stranger was called Emily!

Tremulously, through her tears, Dolly smiled back, and the friendship began.

Buttering a finger of toast on her breakfast plate, Miss Clare mused on that far-distant meeting with the second Emily in her life amid the misery which had engulfed her in the schoolroom. That such 'old, unhappy, far-off things' should have the power to prick her into acute feeling so many years after, made the old lady marvel. Yet, she told herself ruefully, she had difficulty in remembering the name and aspect of a friend's house she had visited only three days earlier! Memory played queer tricks as one grew old.

Emily's face at seventy was far more difficult for her to recall than that seven-year-old's which flashed so vividly upon her inward eye. As for the earlier Emily, who had shared the first six years of her life, why, Miss Clare could see her more clearly still. She could see the brown painted curls, the wide painted eyes and the dented nose which had suffered much banging on floors and chairs. She could smell the stout calico of which she was made, and see the quilted bodice and green-striped long-legged drawers painted upon it; and she could feel even now the delicious scrunch of the hard-packed wood shavings with which she had been stuffed. The sharply indented waist could be spanned by little Dolly's two joined hands, and the legs and arms were prickly at the ends where the calico had worn thin. There was something infinitely reassuring about the smell and weight of Emily as she leant drunkenly against her. No possible harm could befall anyone, thought young Dolly, if Emily were there.

For Emily was the good spirit of the home and, young Dolly felt sure, her blessing embraced Father, Mother, Ada and every living thing in the little house at Caxley where it had all begun so long ago.

CHAPTER 2

IN 1888, the year of Dolly Clare's birth, Caxley was a compact, thriving market town. Its broad main thoroughfare was lined with lime trees and behind these stood shops and private houses built mainly of good rosy brick and weathered tiles.

Here and there, a Georgian front was decorated with grizzled grey bricks known locally as 'vuzz-fired' or 'gorse-fired'. There were several handsome doorways, some hooded, some with elegant fanlights above the well-kept paintwork, and the general impression was one of solid prosperity. Travellers from London, journeying westwards, had paused at Caxley to change horses, or to eat or to sleep, for countless generations and had gone on their way refreshed. There was warmth and beauty in the rose-red aspect of the town and a bustling hospitality among its prosperous tradespeople which won the affection of many a stranger.

The broad High Street narrowed to a stone-built bridge at its western end and crossed a river which wound its placid way to join the Thames. Beyond that, on rising ground to the north, a few cottages constituted the outskirts of the market town, and among these was the four-roomed house belonging to Francis Clare and his young wife.

What the hurrying stranger did not see as he took the highway beyond the handsome bridge was the poorer part of Caxley. The river made its way round the southern part of the town in a series of wide loops. Here was an area of marshland dotted with a few ancient cottages. As the town grew during the nineteenth century, several mean streets were built also on this marshy wasteland by speculators. They were slums within ten years of their building, liable to flooding in the spring and damp from the rising mists for the rest of the year. 'That marsh lot', as the townspeople called them, were scorned, pitied or feared by their more prosperous neighbours, and children from respectable homes were warned against venturing into those narrow streets after dark.

Here lived the humblest of Caxley's citizens. From these dank dwellings, very early each morning, issued the old crones who cleaned steps or scrubbed out shops, the labourers on nearby farms, and those employed in digging a new way for a branch line of the local railway. More often than not there were children left behind in the homes to get what poor breakfast they could before setting out to school. The Education Act of 1870 meant compulsory schooling, and the pennies to pay for it were hard to come by in many a marsh home, and handed over grudgingly on a Monday morning.

But though poverty and hunger, aches and pains were common in these mean streets, conditions were not as stark as in the industrial towns further north and west. Very few children went barefoot and very few older people were callously neglected. Caxley was small enough to know its people, and a rough and ready charity did much to mitigate real need. Though little was organised officially for the relief of the poor in the town, yet shop-keepers, the local gentry and the more prosperous citizens were generous to those in their employ or who were brought to their notice as being in want. This casual and spasmodic generosity had something to commend it in a small community, for the feckless and improvident had small chance of waxing fat at others' expense, while those truly in need were given help. It would take some years before the conscience of the town as a whole was roused by the sight of 'the marsh lot' and their dwellings, but meanwhile they were accepted as 'the poor man at the gate', and an inevitable part of the social structure of any town at that time.

The marsh people themselves frequently said how lucky they were. The parents of some of them had taken part in the bitter riots earlier in the century. The marsh dwellers knew all too well true tales of the starving farm labourers who had marched to demand a wage of half a crown a day, in the winter of 1830. The fate of these unfortunates at their trial, when sentence of death was recorded against many and others were transported as convicts to Australia, was fresh in their memory. Consequently, although their own conditions were deplorable, they considered themselves more fortunate than their predecessors, sharing, to a small extent, the growing prosperity of the latter part of Queen Victoria's long reign.

Perhaps those who felt the pinch most at this time were the small tradesmen, the clerks and the shop assistants, too proud to seek charity, and keeping up an air of respectability with precious little to maintain it. There was a great company of such people in Caxley at that time, dressed in neat, dark attire, much-darned and much-pressed, whose pale faces spoke of long hours and poor nourishment, and whose main anxiety was not so much the serious difficulty of living on their small wages as concealing their difficulties from those about them.

Francis Clare and his wife were of this company. To be sure,

Francis's round face was not pale, for his outdoor occupation gave him a weatherbeaten aspect, but Mary's wore a pinched and sallow look. It was she who bore the major part of their poverty, making each penny do the work of two, and depriving herself so that Francis and the two little girls should benefit.

She had been in good service before her marriage, employed as a general maid in a farmhouse some miles west of Caxley. The farmer and his wife were hard-working and kindly. Despite the low conditions of agriculture at that time, and the recent disastrous harvest of 1870, yet there was wholesome food for all the household produced there. Outside, the logs were stacked in hundreds, sawn up by the farm hands when the weather was too cruel for fieldwork. Coal was cheap and was bought by the truck load. The farm carts trundled to Caxley station once a year bearing sacks of corn, and brought back enough coal for the winter instead.

At Michaelmas the pigs were killed, salted and jointed and hung in clean muslin from the beams in the kitchen. Barley beer was brewed, in an enormous copper, from home-grown barley, and provided a nourishing drink for the men. There was milk in abundance, and butter was made once a week, Mary herself turning the churn more often than not. All the bread, the massive pies and puddings, were made from home-ground wheaten flour. Vegetables and fruit were picked fresh each day from the garden, and the farmhouse kitchen seemed always to be filled with the fragrance and the clatter of cooking.

Only when night came and the oil lamp glowed on the kitchen table, a round pearl of light in its milk-white globe, did the bustle die down. Then the single men, who lived on the premises, and the farmer and his wife, with Mary, quiet as a mouse in the corner, would settle round the fire or at the table, and read or talk or take out the mending basket, until the yawning and nodding began. Then the young men would say

their good-nights before stamping across
the cobbled yard to their bothy above the
stables, and Mary would climb up the
creaking stairs, candle in hand, to her windy
little room under the roof. Finally, the
farmer and his wife would rake through the
fire, put up the massive fire guard, shoot
the heavy bolts on the doors and make
their way to bed. By ten o'clock on a
winter's night the farmhouse would be
wrapped in silent darkness, and the only
sounds to be heard would be the snort and

stamp of a horse beneath the bothy, or the croak of a startled
pheasant from the spinney.

All too soon, it seemed to young Mary, the morning would
come, and she would hear the carters taking their horses across
the yard, the rumble of heavy wheels and the rhythmic
squeak from the pump handle in the yard as the farm hands
set about their work. Soon, she too would have to clamber
from her truckle bed to rekindle the great kitchen fire, the first
of many jobs.

The days were long and busy. Mary learnt how to keep a
house clean, to cook and to sew. The farmer and his wife were
childless and treated Mary with affection. She was a docile girl,
willing to learn and fond of her employers. Life at the farm was
hard but happy, and no doubt she would have been content to
stay there for many years had Francis Clare not crossed her path.

He was twenty years of age when first she saw him. He came
in the early autumn, with his father, to thatch the six great ricks
of wheat and barley which stood majestically in a nearby field.
His hair glinted as brightly as the straw among which he stood
and his blue eyes appraised Mary as she carried an earthenware
jug of tea to the thatchers. The two men were at work there

for a week, and Francis made no secret of his interest in Mary.

Later that autumn he came again, this time alone, to repair the thatch on one of the barns. He appeared so often at the kitchen door, and Mary seemed to have so many occasions to cross the yard to the barn during his stay, that she was sorely teased. The farmer and his wife liked young Francis. He and his father were known for miles around as respectable and honest workers. There was no reason in the world why Mary should not welcome the young man's advances. There would always be work for a thatcher, they told each other, and they could not keep a good girl like Mary, now almost twenty and as pretty as ever she would be, on a lonely farm for ever.

By Christmas it was generally understood that Francis and Mary were 'keeping company'. Now Mary's needlework was for her trousseau and her bottom drawer. The farmer's wife, when sorting out her linen or her crockery would say:

'Here, my dear, put that aside with your things. 'Tis a bit shabby, maybe, but it'll prove useful, I don't doubt.' Later, Mary was to count these casual gifts amongst her dearest possessions.

On Michaelmas Day in the following year Mary was married to Francis and the young couple went to live in the little house on the outskirts of Caxley. They paid a rent of two shillings a week to the baker in Caxley who owned the property. Francis had ten pounds in savings, and Mary had five new golden sovereigns, a wedding present from the farmer and his wife. There was plenty of work to be had. Francis owned a fine set of thatching tools and had abundant strength and skill to use them. Queen Victoria had reigned for almost fifty years, England was beginning to enjoy prosperity, and Francis and Mary, young and in love, prepared to be as happy as larks as the year 1885 drew to its close.

*　　　*　　　*

Mary Clare's first home was one of a pair of cottages close to the road which ran northwards from Caxley. Francis's own home lay less than a mile away, and his parents were frequent visitors.

A narrow strip of garden lay between the road and the front door, and the little brick path was edged with large white stones. This tiny patch Mary claimed for her own and busily planted pinks and columbines and a great clump of old-fashioned purple iris to flower the next year. A moss-rose already flourished by the gate, and still bore a late bloom or two when Mary arrived at the house as a bride.

The front door led directly into the main living-room of the house, and behind this was a small scullery. A box staircase led from the living-room to the main bedroom at the front of the house, and a narrow slip room, above the scullery, which was really nothing more than an extension of the minute landing, constituted the second bedroom.

It was a small house, but enough for the young couple, and they arranged their few pieces of furniture to the best advantage and were well content. Mary's taste was good. Her own home, a farm labourer's cottage, had been humble but beautifully clean and neat, and at the farmhouse she was accustomed to seeing solid pieces of well-made furniture, and well-designed utensils of copper and wood in daily use.

She spread the scrubbed deal table with a red serge cloth in the afternoons, when the midday meal was done, and enjoyed the sight of a white geranium in a pot set squarely upon it. Round the edge ran fringed bobbles which were to delight her little daughters in the years to come. On the mantelpiece stood bright tins containing sugar, currants, tea and salt. The rag rug before the hearth was of her own making, and the fender and fire-irons of steel were polished first thing every morning with a small square of emery paper, until they shone as brightly as silver.

Their only regret was the smallness of the garden. Only a few yards of light soil stretched beyond the back doors of the two cottages.

'Not enough to keep us in potatoes,' said Francis, 'let alone a bit of green stuff.'

He planted onions, carrots and a row of cottagers' kale, and set down some old flagstones near the back door for Mary's wood and iron mangle to stand upon. This done, there was no room for anything else in the garden.

To have to buy vegetables seemed shocking to the young couple, and certainly an unnecessary expense. As the first few months went by Mary was appalled to find how much it cost to run even such a modest establishment as their own.

Not only vegetables, but meat, eggs, flour and fruit, which had been so abundant at the farm, and which she had hitherto taken for granted, now had to be bought at the shops in Caxley High Street or at the market. Despite her care, Mary found that she frequently had to ask Francis for more housekeeping money, and she began to dread the look of anxiety that crossed his face when she told him that she had no money left in her shabby purse.

For the truth of the matter was that Francis was even more discomfited by the cost of married life than his wife. Although there was always thatching to be done, yet it tended to be seasonal work. After harvest, when the ricks needed to be thatched, the money came in well; but in the winter time when bad weather made work impossible, a thatcher might go for weeks with no earnings.

Francis was beginning to find, too, that the customers who had employed both his father and himself now tended to ask his father alone to do their work. It had been agreed between them, at the time of Francis's marriage, that they would set up separately, and it was only natural that the older man should

be asked first to undertake those jobs which he had done for
many years. There was no doubt, too, that Francis was not as
skilful or as quick as his father. He began to find that he had a
serious rival here, and though they were outwardly as devoted
as ever, yet Francis could not help feeling that his own trade
was decreasing steadily while his father's prospered.

He took to going further afield for work, and set out very
early to any job he had been lucky enough to get. Clad in thick
clothes, wearing heavy hob-nailed boots and leather leggings,
he trudged off, before daybreak during the first winter, along
the muddy lanes to the north and west of Caxley. He had built
himself a little handcart in which he pushed the tools of his
trade, his shears, roofing knife, eaves knife, twine, and the
bundles of short hazel strips, called sprays in those parts, which
were bent in two and used as staples to hold down the thatch.

There were many hazel thickets on the chalky slopes around
Caxley, and Francis had permission to cut from several of
them. Mary used to enjoy these outings to collect the hazel
sticks, and never came back without a few flowers or berries
from the woods to decorate the window sill. Later she used to
help Francis to slice the sticks and to sharpen each end so that
the straw would be pierced easily.

Despite the pinch of poverty, the two were happy, although
neither of them enjoyed living so near to a town, and Mary
missed the boisterous friendliness of the farmhouse. Although
she did not admit it to her husband, she found life in the cottage
lonely. Her immediate neighbours were an aged couple, both
deaf and quarrelsome, who had rebuffed her innocent country-
bred advances when she first arrived. She was too timid to do
more, and knew no one of her own age in Caxley.

Consequently, she was obliged to fall back upon her own
resources during the long days when Francis was away from
home. She scoured and scrubbed, cooked and sewed in the

little house, and worried constantly about making ends meet. She was determined not to lower her standards and become like 'that marsh lot' who lived within a mile of her own doorstep. She had lost her way among those dank streets one day when she was exploring the town, and had been distressed and frightened by the dirt and violence she saw there. In the first few months of married life Mary adopted an attitude of proud respectability which was to remain for the rest of her life.

In the summer of 1886 their first child was born. The baby arrived during one of the hottest spells in August, a small, compact child, fair like her father, and as neat and beautiful as a doll. Francis and Mary were delighted. She was christened Ada Mary and throve from the first.

'But it's to be a boy next time,' said Francis, bouncing his little daughter on his knee. 'Must have another thatcher in the family, or who's to carry on when I'm past it?'

'I'll see what I can do,' promised Mary.

But it was not to be. When Ada was rising two, a fat toddler already tugging the fringed bobbles from the red tablecloth, a second daughter arrived.

It was an April day. This second birth was more complicated than the first, and Mary had paced the little bedroom all day, watching the showers sweeping across the window and drenching the primroses in the tiny front garden.

It was early evening when the baby was born. The showers suddenly stopped, and the sinking sun lit up the room with golden brilliance.

'Open the window,' whispered the mother to the old woman who acted as midwife.

The cool breeze carried with it the fragrance of wet earth and spring flowers. On the glistening rose-bush a thrush sang his heart out, welcoming the sun after the storm.

' 'Tis a good omen,' pronounced the old crone, returning to the bedside. ' That'll be a lucky baby, just you wait and see.'

'But it's a girl!' cried Mary, tears of weakness springing to her eyes at the thought of Francis's disappointment when the news should reach him.

'That don't matter,' replied the old woman sturdily. 'That child be blessed, I tell you, boy or girl. And the day will come when you'll remember what I told you.'

Mary need not have worried. Francis welcomed this second little girl as warmly as the first. Although she had not the beauty, nor the lusty strength of Ada, she was equally fair, and very much quieter in temperament.

One Sunday afternoon in May, when all the lilac was in flower and Mary's clump of irises hung out their purple flags, the Clare family, dressed in their best clothes, carried the baby to the parish church. She wore the same long christening robe which Ada had worn, a garment of fine white lawn, made by Mary, covered with innumerable tucks and edged with hand-made crochet work.

Mary felt a glow of pride as she handed this elegant bundle to the vicar at the font.

'I name this child Dorothy Annie,' intoned the vicar sonorously, and dipped his finger in the water.

CHAPTER 3

MEMORIES of her first home crowded back to Miss Clare as she cleared her breakfast table in the kitchen at Beech Green. To be sure, she thought, the things that one would have expected to see most clearly escaped her. The faces of her mother and father, the aspect of the home outside and the simple geography of its interior, the view of the lane seen through the wooden palings of the gate, and even the appearance of her sister Ada at that time, evaded her memory.

And yet there were other things, objects of no particular merit or beauty, whose feel and smell – and taste, too, in some cases – she recalled with a thrilling clarity after all these years. The white stone nearest the wooden front gate, the first of the row leading to the door, was particularly beloved by little Dolly. It rose to a substantial knob, large enough for a small foot to balance on, and so afforded her a better view of the world outside the front garden. At the foot of the knob was a hole, about two inches across, which held rainwater to the depth of a child's finger. It glittered in the whiteness like a grey eye in a pale face, and gave the stone its individuality. Sometimes the child propped a flower in this natural vase, a daisy or a violet, and once she had dropped in one of the scurrying wood lice which lived beneath the shelter of the stone. The pathetic attempts of the creature to climb out, and her own remorse when it died in the hollow of her palm, were never forgotten.

There was, too, a certain knot in the wood of the back door whose satin smoothness Miss Clare could still feel on her finger tip. Below it a drop of resin had exuded, sticky and aromatic. These two fascinating lumps, one cold and hard, the other warm and soft, within an inch of each other, were a source of wonder and joy to the child. Nearby was the handle of her mother's heavy mangle, white as a bone with drenchings of soap and water, and split here and there so deeply that a child could insert tiny leaves and twigs and make believe that she was posting letters.

Other memories were as fresh. Miss Clare recalled the slippery coldness of the steel fire-irons beneath her small hand, the delicious stuffy secrecy of hiding beneath the table, and the sight of the red bobbles quivering at the edge of the tablecloth. She could still feel the mingled love and terror which shook her when her father held her high above his head near to the oil-lamp that swung from the ceiling, and the roughness of his coat and the prickliness of his cheek.

But clearer than any of these early memories was that of Emily the doll. Heavy, ungainly, battered, but ineffably dear, the look, smell, feel and taste of her rag doll flashed back across the years to Miss Clare. Her home and her family might be hidden by the mists of time, but the image of Emily shone still, as splendid as a star.

*   *   *

With the arrival of her second child Mary Clare found her life busier than ever. Throughout the summer of 1888 she struggled against an overpowering weariness. As was the custom at that time, the young mother had fed her first baby for over a year, and prepared to do the same with the second. But poor diet and the constant nagging worry of making ends meet had taken their toll. Little Dolly's progress was slower than her lusty sister's had been, and Mary faced the unpleasant fact that she would have to stop feeding the child herself and undertake the expense of buying milk for its consumption. It was a bitter blow.

With the coming of autumn Mary's spirits sank still further. Now came the added expense of coal, oil and candles, winter boots for Francis and warmer clothes for the children. She spoke despairingly to her husband, and he did his best to cheer her. His was a resilient nature, the open air blew away his cares, and he had no idea of the intensity of his wife's misery cooped up in the little house with her babies and with nothing to deflect her mind from the cares around her.

'You let me do the worrying, gal,' he told her with rough affection. 'I guaranteed to look after you when we was wed, and I'll do it, never you fear!'

He gazed round the lamp-lit room, at the firelight glinting on the polished fender and the black pot which bubbled on the hob sending out wafts of boiling bacon. Upstairs his daughters lay asleep, bonny and beautiful. He could see no reason why Mary fretted so.

'We may be a bit short – but that's only natural. We're in no debt, and now the harvest's in there's work aplenty for me. We'll be able to put something by this winter, for sure, then one day we'll be able to get somewhere further out in the country to live. Be better for you up on the downs, I reckon. 'Tis lowering to the spirits, living near the marsh here.'

Mary did her best to be comforted. She had not the energy
to point out the drawbacks of the little house, nor did she want
to appear dissatisfied with the home that Francis had provided.
Compared with 'the marsh lot' they were superbly housed, but
the autumn gales had lifted several slates from the roof and had
driven rain into the bedroom through the gaps. The window
frames had shrunk with age and fitted poorly, and many a keen
draught whistled through the rooms. There was no damp
course, and the walls of the scullery glistened with moisture. The
strip of matting which Mary spread on the flag-stoned floor
there was dank and smelt musty.

Francis was a handy man and cheerfully undertook household repairs. It was as well that he did, for the baker landlord in
Caxley took no interest in his property at all. He knew, though
his tenants did not, that the pair of cottages was to be de-
molished within a year or two to make way for an extension of
the railway line already being prepared from Caxley to the
northern part of the county. He did not intend to spend
another penny on his houses, and told Francis so flatly when the
young man timidly approached him.

'What d'you expect for two shilluns a week?' growled the
baker. 'A palace? And how far d'you reckon two shilluns is
going to go when it comes to putting a new set of slates on the
roof? You wants to come down to earth, me boy. If that ain't
grand enough for you, you knows the answer.'

After this encounter, Francis was even more determined to
move house as soon as he could find somewhere that he could
afford. Meanwhile he and Mary stuffed the cracks with folded
paper, and Francis borrowed a ladder and did a little rough
thatching here and there among the slates of the rickety roof, to
keep the worst of the weather out.

Mary stuffed long strips of sacking with more straw, and put
these sausages along the foot of the outside doors which let in

the fiercest draughts. They were makeshift measures, but they helped to make the little house more habitable, and gave the young couple a comfortable glow of self-reliance, despite their poverty.

'Where there's a will there's a way!' quoted Mary, ramming a draught-stopper hard against the lintel.

'We'll find somewhere by the spring,' promised Francis, glad to see a momentary return of her spirits.

But his brave hopes were doomed to be dashed. The winter of 1888 still lay ahead, and worse troubles than poverty were to visit the Clares' home during those bitter months.

One November morning, soon after his encounter with the landlord, Francis Clare was at work for another landlord, more zealous than his own.

His employer on this occasion was a man called Jesse Miller, who farmed several hundred acres of land lying between Beech Green and Springbourne. He was reckoned to be a hard man of business but a good master to his men. He had more conscience than many of his fellow farmers at that time, and saw to it that his men were housed well. To be hired by Jesse Miller at the Michaelmas hiring fair in Caxley meant hard work but above average living conditions, as the local workers knew well.

Francis was busy thatching a long row of four cottages, and expected to finish the work by the end of that particular week. The day in question was clear and sparkling, and from his lofty perch Francis had a fine view of the distant downs, a soft blue hump against the bluer sky. A clump of elm trees at the edge of Hundred Acre Field had turned a vivid yellow, and reminded Francis of the sprigs of cauliflower, stained with turmeric, that were to be found in his wife's home-made piccalilli.

The sun was overhead, and his stomach told him that it was

dinner time long before the clock on Beech Green church struck twelve. He descended the ladder and fetched his satchel from the handcart.

Seated on a bank, at the rear of the cottages, he enjoyed the warm sunshine on his face. He undid the knot of the red and white spotted handkerchief that held his meal and took out a generous cube of fat boiled bacon, the heel of a cottage loaf, and a small raw onion.

He ate slowly, paring the food into small pieces with his old worn clasp-knife. A tame bantam sidled closer as the meal progressed, looking with a sharp speculative eye at the feast. Now and again Francis tossed her a crumb which she pecked up swiftly, and afterwards she would emit little hoarse cooing noises, half purr and half croak, in the hope of further largesse.

He heard the click of a gate at the front of the cottages and guessed that one of the men was coming in for his midday meal. The appetising smell of rabbit stew from the end cottage had tickled his nostrils most of the morning. Only one other cottage was occupied that day, by an old lady whose son was working on a distant quarter of the farm. Two younger women from the other two cottages had gone together by the carrier's cart to Caxley market.

Although Francis Clare knew pretty well all that was going on in the houses upon which he was engaged, he made it a rule to be as unobtrusive as possible. His father had taught him the wisdom of such conduct many years before.

'People don't want you prying into their affairs,' the old man had said. 'You be enough nuisance anyway, sitting atop their roof days on end. And there's another side to it. Say you gets chatting one day, come the next the women'll come chatting to you when you wants to get on – or, worse still, asking you to chop 'em a bit of firing or mend the clothes line. You keep yourself to yourself, my boy, and get on with your own job.'

It had been good advice, thought Francis, putting the last piece of bread in his mouth, and leaning back for a brief rest. He closed his eyes against the dazzle of the sun. The food made him content and drowsy, and for two pins, he told himself, he could doze off. But the days were short, there were still a few yards of roof to thatch, and he must get back to the job. He stood up briskly, brushing the crumbs from his thick corduroy trousers, observed the while by the attentive bantam.

He was halfway up the ladder, emerging from the shadow of the cottage into the bright sunlight on the roof, when the accident happened. His heavy boot slipped on a rung, he lunged sideways to catch at the roof, missed his hold, and crashed to the ground, with one leg trapped in the ladder which fell across him.

The noise brought the labourer and his wife running from their back door, and the old crone, who lived next door, hobbling after them. They found Francis, with his eyes closed, blood oozing from a gash at the temple, and his left leg bent at an unusual angle, and still threaded through the ladder.

"E be dead!' said the old woman flatly. She took off her apron calmly and began to spread it over the unconscious face of Francis.

With some exasperation her neighbour twitched it off.

'Give 'im time,' begged John Arnold roughly. "E's winded, that's all. Cut back and get a drop of water, gal,' he commanded his wife.

Francis Clare came round to feel the sting of cold water upon his forehead, the blue sky above him, and an over-powering smell of rabbit stew blowing upon his face from the anxious countenances that bent over him.

'Take it easy, mate,' said John Arnold kindly. 'You bin and done a bit of damage to your leg. We'll lift you inside.'

'You looked dead to me,' quavered the old lady. She sounded

disappointed. 'Cut down like grass, you was. White as a shroud. I said to John 'ere: "'E's dead!" Didn't I then, John? I thought you was, you see,' she explained, her silver head nodding and shaking like a poplar leaf.

The journey from the hard earth to the rickety sofa in John Arnold's living-room seemed the longest one of Francis's life. He lay there with sweat running down his ashen face, listening to the three making plans for him.

'I'll run up to Mr Miller. He'll know what's best, and meantime you get on up to Doctor's and see if he be home to his dinner,' said John, taking command. 'And you, granny, bide here with the poor chap and see he don't move. Come 'e do, he'll have them bone ends ground together or set all ways. That wants setting straight again in a splint, but us'll do more harm than good to meddle.'

He turned to Francis and patted his shoulder encouragingly.

'Don't fear now. We'll be back afore you knows where you are.'

'But you haven't had your dinner!' protested Francis weakly, looking at the plates which steamed upon the table.

'That don't matter,' said John heartily, and disappeared through the door, followed by his wife who tugged on her coat as she ran.

Francis heard their hurrying footsteps fade away and thought how good people were to each other. John must be hungry, his wife had spent all the morning preparing that savoury dish, yet not a flicker of reproach had crossed their faces at this interruption. Their only concern was for his comfort.

The old lady had turned a chair sideways to the table and sat with one elbow on the scrubbed top, gazing at him with dark beady eyes.

Francis smiled weakly at her, but his head throbbed so violently and he felt so giddy that he was unable to talk to her.

He closed his eyes and listened to the whisper of the fire in the kitchen range and the rhythmic wheezing of the old woman's breathing. Within two minutes he had fallen asleep.

The doctor could not be found. He was still out on his rounds, rattling along the country lanes in his gig, and not likely to be back until well after dark, his wife said.

Francis was carried back to his home in one of Jesse Miller's carts. A bed of straw and sacks lessened the jolting, but the deeply rutted road caused many a sickening lurch and Francis could have wept with relief when the cart stopped at his gate and John Arnold went in to break the news to Mary.

For almost three months Francis was unable to go to work, growing more anxious and dispirited as December made way for January and the weather grew more bitter. It was now Mary's turn to comfort, and this she did as well as she could.

Lack of money was their immediate problem, for with the bread winner useless nothing came into the house. Francis's father came forward at once and insisted on doing his son's outstanding work as well as his own, handing over the money to Francis and waving his thanks aside. Francis and Mary never forgot their debt to his parents, and the two couples were more closely knit by this misfortune than ever before.

The kindly farmer and his wife, from whose house Mary had been married, heard of her plight and sent a bundle of mending for Mary to do weekly, and paid her for it very generously. The carrier's cart brought the mending, and a big basket of vegetables, eggs and butter as well, and such kindnesses warmed their sad hearts during that cold winter.

Sometimes, in his blackest moods of inaction, Francis would brood on the unjust state of affairs which cast a man still further into despair when he needed help most. He was grateful to his father, to his friends and neighbours, but he did not want charity. Somehow or other he ought to be able to ensure that a certain amount of money came into his home to keep his wife and babies while he was off work. People talked about it, he knew. It was to be a long time before such theories were put into practice, and meanwhile Francis and his wife had to endure hard times.

In later years Dolly Clare was to hear her parents talk of that black winter, the first of her life, as the time when they had been driven to the verge of despair.

But time passed, the spring came, and Francis limped about again, burning to get back to work. Mary's spirits rose, Ada played once more in the little garden, and the baby lay there too in its wicker bassinet, gazing at this bright new world and finding it good.

CHAPTER 4

THE baby's first birthday was celebrated by a family picnic in the woods which bordered an expanse of common land north of Caxley.

After the bitter winter, spring was doubly welcome. It was unusually warm. Primroses and anemones starred the leafy mould underfoot, and early bluebells, still knotted in bud, were already to be seen. Mary and Francis breathed in the woodland scents hungrily as they rested on a mossy bank with their backs against the rough comfort of a beech tree.

The battered baby carriage was drawn up nearby, its occupant deep in sleep. But Ada, rosy and sturdy, scrambled joyfully over tree roots, plucking the heads from flowers and gathering twigs, feathers, acorn cups, pebbles and any other fascinating object which caught her excited eye.

'Wouldn't it be lovely,' said Mary dreamily, observing the child's happiness, 'to have a little house of our own in this wood. Or better still, just on the edge of it, on the common.'

Francis smiled at her fancies.

'We'd soon be hustled off, I knows,' he told her. 'No better'n gipsies, we'd be thought. But you take heart, my dear, one of these fine days you shall have a little house away from Caxley and the throng.'

With the sun above him, the warm air lifting his bright hair, and his family closely about him, Francis felt his strength renewed. He had been back at work for some weeks, and although his injured leg was still weak he found that he could get through a day's work steadily. Although money was scarce, to be busy again raised the young man's spirits. In a month's time, he told himself, his leg would be as good as new. In fact, it was never to be quite as strong as its fellow, and Francis walked with a slight limp for the rest of his life.

Mary stirred from her day-dreaming and began to unpack the food from the basket. Ada, breathless with her exertions, came up to this interesting object, and flung herself down beside her mother.

'I wonder where we'll all be this time next year,' said Mary, holding a loaf to her chest and looking across its crusty top to the distant common. 'D'you reckon we'll have that little house by the time our Dolly's two years old?'

'That we will!' promised her husband stoutly. 'Just you wait and see!'

But Mary was to wait for another five years before hope of a country cottage came her way, and little Dolly was to celebrate several birthdays at Caxley before making her home in the Beech Green cottage which would shelter her for the rest of her long life.

*   *   *

It was in Caxley, therefore, that Dolly Clare spent the first
formative years of her life. The lane outside the cottage gate
was dusty in summer and clogged with mud in the winter. The
child watched the carts and waggons, the carriages of the
gentry and the tradesmen's vans, rumble and rattle on their
way, raising dust or churning mud, as they travelled to and
from the town. The diversity of the horses fascinated her. Ada
loved best the shiny high-stepping carriage horses that trotted
proudly past, and would call excitedly to her little sister when
she saw them approaching:

'Come quick, Doll! Quick, you'll miss 'em!'

But Dolly's favourites were the slow-moving patient great
cart horses whose shaggy hooves stirred vast clouds of dust as

they plodded towards the market town with the farm waggons thundering behind them. There was a humility and a nobility about these powerful monsters which tore at the young child's heart in a way which she could not express, but which was to remain with her always.

The two little girls reacted differently to many things. To go shopping in the High Street or in the market square was a delight to the volatile Ada. To the quieter Dolly it was sheer misery.

'Ada! Dolly!' The urgent summons from the house in their mother's voice would be the prelude to this ordeal.

First they had to endure a brisk rubbing of hands and faces with a soapy flannel wrung out in cold water. Then came swift and painful combing of hair with a steel comb which seemed to find out every sensitive spot on little Dolly's scalp. Both children had curly hair. Ada's sprang crisply from her head, but Dolly's was softer and fell in loose curls, later to form ringlets. Ada endured the hair-tugging stoically, chattering the while about what she would see and what she wanted her mother to buy.

'Hold still, child!' Mary would command. 'And hush your tongue! Us'll be lucky to get a good dinner from the shops, let alone sweeties and dollies and picture books!'

Dolly's eyes filled with tears of pain during the combing, despite Mary's endeavour to handle her gently. She knew it was no pleasure for the younger child to go shopping, but there was no one to mind her and the two must perforce accompany their mother everywhere.

At last they set out. Sometimes Dolly was pushed in the rickety perambulator, but its days were numbered, and more often than not she would struggle along beside her mother's long heavy skirt, clutching it with one desperate hand, or holding on to the stout shopping basket which her mother held.

Never for a moment did she let go. The thought of being parted from her mother was too terrifying to be borne.

Ada, on the other side, leapt and gambolled as gaily as a young goat, greeting friends, pointing out anything which caught her eye – a lady's pink parasol, a gleaming carriage door with a crest on it, or a pig squealing in a cart, covered with a stout net, and resenting every minute of its journey to the market.

Caxley High Street was always busy. It was a thriving town which served a large area, and the shops always had far too many hurrying people in them for little Dolly's liking. Customers pressed up to the counters to be served, assistants scurried back and forth filling baskets, weighing out sugar, fetching lumps of yellow butter on wooden pats, and slapping them feverishly into shape on the marble slab behind the counter.

Important customers usually waited in their carriages outside the shop while their menservants bustled to and fro carrying parcels, and the proprietor of the business himself fetched and carried too, leaving his premises to pay his respects at the carriage side. Sometimes a horseman, not wishing to dismount, would shout his order to someone in the shop. Out would race the shop boy at top speed, the parcel would be stuffed into a jacket pocket, coins would jingle, and the horse would clop-clop off down the street again.

The bustle was the breath of life to Ada. She scrambled up on the high round-seated chair by each counter, bouncing with such zest that her lofty ill-balanced perch frequently tipped over. From here she watched, with eyes as bright and round as a squirrel's. She loved to see the butter patted, and its final adornment with a swan or a crown from the heavy wooden butter-stamp. She delighted in the scooping of currants from deep drawers with a shiny shovel, and the see-sawing of the gold-bright scales and weights.

But Dolly, crouched between the counter and her mother's

skirt, was in no mood to relish these joys. Bewildered by the noise, hustled to one side if she ventured forth, and half-suffocated by the people who pressed and towered around her, she longed for the time when her mother replaced her purse in the deep petticoat pocket beneath her voluminous skirts and they could make their way out into the street again.

Of all the shops, Dolly dreaded most the butcher's. The headless carcases, split down the middle to disclose heaven knew what nameless horrors in their sinister depths, were frightening enough. The poor dangling hares, with blood dripping from their noses to the sawdust on the floor, were infinitely worse. To see them flung on to the butcher's block and to watch his red hands wrenching the skins, with a sickening tearing sound, from their bodies was even more terrifying to the child, and the final awful tugging to release the head had once caused her to be sick upon the sawdust, thus bringing upon herself the wrath of her mother and the butcher combined.

But the most appalling experience, which happened all too frequently, was the purchase of half a pig's head. This useful piece of meat was very cheap and very nutritious, and Mary Clare often bought it for her family. Dolly watched, with fascinated horror, the whole head placed upon the butcher's block. The eyes, small and blue in death, seemed to look at her. There was something pitiful and lovable about its round rubbery nose and the cock of its great waxen ears. When the butcher, chatting cheerfully the while, raised his cleaver, Dolly squeezed her eyes shut and gritted her milk teeth, remaining so until the ominous thudding had stopped. She had never been able to keep her eyes closed long enough for the butcher to weigh, trim and wrap the meat, and so endured each time the ghastly sight of that cloven head, brains, tongue and grinning teeth exposed by the butcher's onslaught.

Mary, delighting in her purchase and making plans for several meals from it, never knew the repugnance which little Dolly felt. The child could not go near the basket which held this horror, shrouded in newspaper, and was careful to walk on the other side of her mother on the return journey. For Dolly, this was only the beginning of her misery. The pig's head would float, she knew well, in a basin of brine for hours to come, on the floor of the scullery, and every movement would set it swivelling slowly, while one blue eye cast a cold malevolent beam from its watery resting-place.

'Don't pick at your vittles,' Mary would say two days later, when she placed a plate of boiled pig's brain before her younger daughter. 'Look at Ada gobbling up hers! You be a good girl, now, and clean up your plate.'

'That's right, my little love,' Francis would say jovially. 'Thousands of poor children 'ud give their eye teeth for a plate-ful of brains like that. Why, I wager there's plenty down the marsh would like 'em!'

For all unhappy little Dolly cared, as she pushed the revolting things about, the marsh children could have them. Memories of the butcher's shop, the strain of living with half a pig's head in the house, and meeting the reproachful gaze of that one fear-some eye, completely robbed Dolly of any appetite. Her parents' concern was an added burden, yet how could she explain her revulsion?

And so the pigs' heads continued to appear and to cast their shadow over young Dolly's existence. It was small wonder that shopping in Caxley High Street presented so little attraction for the child in her early years.

Although Dolly's heart sank when her mother slammed the gate and turned left towards the town, it rose with equal speed if she turned to the right, for that way lay the fields, woods and gorsy common land which were becoming so dear to her. That way led to her grandparents' home. Most visiting was done on a Sunday, when Francis was free.

During his enforced idleness, and as soon as he could hobble as far, it had become a habit for the young family to spend Sundays with the old people.

'At least they'll get a good feed,' old Mrs Clare had told her husband. 'That baby don't appear too strong, for my liking; and it takes Francis out of himself to leave that chair of his now and again.'

'Don't overdo it,' advised her husband. 'They don't like to feel they're having charity, that pair, and good luck to 'em. Besides, they won't want Sundays booked here for the rest of their lives. Invite 'em as much as you like while things are bad – but you ease up a bit when our Francis is back at work.'

By the time the little girls were four and six, the Sunday visits were occasional treats. One particular Sunday remained vividly in Miss Clare's memory.

It was a day of high summer. The family set off clad in their Sunday best. Francis wore the dark suit which he had bought for his wedding, and Mary's lilac print was drawn back into a bustle showing a darker mauve skirt below. Three rows of purple velvet ribbon edged the skirt, and on her head was a neat straw hat with velvet pansies to match the underskirt. Both frock and hat had been a present from her generous employers at the time of her wedding, and were kept carefully shrouded in a piece of sheeting on working days. Dolly thought her mother looked wonderful as they set off, and told her so.

'Has Queen Victoria got a hat like that?' she wanted to know.

'Dozens of 'em,' laughed her mother, flattered nevertheless by the child's admiration.

'Not as pretty,' maintained Dolly stoutly. Her own clothes

did not give her as much pleasure. Her two petticoats, lace-edged drawers and white muslin frock had been so stiffly starched that it had been necessary to tear them apart before arms and legs could be inserted. Now the prickly edges dug into her tender flesh, and she knew from experience that the lace on her drawers would print strange and uncomfortable patterns on her thighs from the pressure against grandma's horsehair sofa. Tucked under one arm she held Emily, wrapped in a piece of one of her own old shawls. She was the least well-dressed of the party, but not in her mistress's eyes. She was heavy, too, and Dolly was obliged to hitch her up every few yards.

But these minor discomforts were soon forgotten in the joys of the walk. They crossed a stile and made their way across a meadow high with summer grass. Some of the bobbing grasses stood as high as Dolly herself and she saw, for the first time, the tiny mauve seeds quivering at the grass tips. Ox-eyed daisies and red sorrel lit this sweet-smelling jungle that stretched as far as the small child could see. Above her arched a sky of breath-taking blue where two larks vied with each other in their outpourings.

In the distance the six bells of Caxley parish church chased each other's tails madly. A warm breeze, scented with the perfume from a field of beans in flower, lifted Dolly's hair, and she became aware, young as she was, of her own happiness in these surroundings. Sunlight, flowers, Mother, Father, Ada, and dear Emily were with her. Here was security, warmth, love and life. Nothing ever completely dimmed that shining memory.

At grandma's house there were different joys. There was an aura of comfort and well-being here which the child sensed at once. The furniture was old and solid, unlike the poorer machine-made products in her own home. The old couple had inherited well-made pieces from their families, and the patina of a century's polishing gleamed upon the woodwork. These sturdy chairs and chests had been made and used long before the commons were enclosed and their self-supporting owners became poor men. The difference in the two homes was eloquent testimony to the revolution which had split a nation into classes. Although the young Clares might consider themselves fortunate when they compared their way of life with that of 'the marsh lot', yet the fact remained that they were as poor. Francis's parents were the last inheritors of an older England where a man might live, modestly but freely, off his own bit of ground.

After the greetings and the Sunday dinner were over, the grown-ups settled back to rest and talk and the two children were told to sit up to the table to play.

'I'll take off your sashes, so they don't get crushed,' said their mother, undoing Ada's blue and Dolly's pink ones. It was good to expand, free of their bindings. The sashes were eight inches wide and four or five feet long. Made of stout ribbed silk, they were considerably restricting when tied tightly round a well-filled stomach. Dolly watched with relief as her mother rolled them up, smoothing them on the table to take away the wrinkles.

Ada was given a picture book, but Dolly had her favourite object to play with – a square tin with pictures of Queen Victoria on each side. It had been bought at the time of the sovereign's golden jubilee, the year before Dolly's birth, and had held tea then. Now it was grandma's button box, and Dolly was allowed to spill out the contents across the table and count them, or form them into patterns, or match them, or simply gloat over their diversity of beauty.

There were big ones and tiny ones. Buttons from coats and caps, from pillowcases and pinafores, from bonnets and boots, cascaded across the table. There were buttons made of horn, bone, cut steel, jet, mother o'pearl, linen and leather. Dolly's fingertips, as well as her excited eyes, experienced the gamut of sensations roused by handling the variety of sizes, textures, colours and shapes which were held in the bright button box.

As she bent over her treasures, scraps of conversation floated to her from the grown-ups.

'Found a house yet, my boy?'

'Not that I can afford, Dad.'

'You won't find anything much cheaper than your own, I'd say. Take my advice and stay on a bit till you've built up the work again.'

'Things aren't too good. Straw's scarce.'

'Ah, there's not the wheat grown. Old George Jackson, shepherd to Jesse Miller, was in here this week. He's got more sheep than ever before. He gets twelve shilluns a week, he tells me, and two pounds Michaelmas money. He's not doing so bad.'

'And gets it regular, too,' said young Francis, with a hint of bitterness in his voice.

The women talked of clothes and bed-linen, meals and children. They seemed, to Dolly, to talk of nothing else, unless it were of illness and death, and then it was in low tones meant to keep such things from attentive young ears.

At last the time came when the buttons must be swept from the table back into the jingling tin. Dolly followed the two women into the kitchen and watched the preparations for tea.

Bread and butter at grandma's was quite different from that at home, for here the bread was cut very thin and buttered very thickly. Home-made plum jam could be spread upon the second slice, too – the first must be eaten plain – whereas at home one either had bread with butter on it or bread with jam, never both. Fingers of sponge cake followed the bread and

butter, the top sparkling with a generous sprinkling of sugar.

The children had milk to drink from mugs with a pattern of ivy leaves round the rim, but the grown-ups had tea poured from a huge brown tea-pot which wore a snug buttoned jacket to keep the tea hot.

Grandma's tea was kept in a shiny wooden tea-caddy with a brass lion's head for a handle on the lid. When this was lifted, Dolly saw first two bowls filled with sugar, each settled securely in a hole. At each side of the caddy lay a long polished lid with a small black knob. When these were lifted they disclosed the tea, China on one side, and Indian on the other. This tea-caddy was an unfailing joy to Dolly, and when later it came into her possession she treasured it as much for its intrinsic beauty as for its associations.

After tea the little girls' sashes were re-tied, their hair combed and their hands and faces washed upstairs in grandma's bedroom. The thick eaves of the thatch jutted out beyond the windows and made the room seem dark, despite the golden evening.

Then came the moment which was to stamp this particular Sunday as a day of perfection as clearly as the morning walk through the meadow had done.

The old lady opened a drawer in the chest by the bed and took out a piece of red flannel.

'For Emily,' she said, giving it to Dolly.

The child unfolded the material slowly and with some bewilderment. It proved to be a cloak with a hood, exactly the right size for the doll.

Dolly was speechless with joy. She could do nothing but throw her arms round her grandmother's knees and press her flushed face against the black silk of the old lady's Sunday frock.

'Well, what do you say?' said Mary with increasing asperity. But Dolly could say nothing. With trembling hands she unbound the shawl from Emily' heavy body and dressed her in her new finery. She looked even lovelier than her mother had looked that morning, and far more splendid than Queen Victoria on the side of the button box.

'I made it out of my old petticoat,' said grandma, as they descended the steep stairs. 'There wasn't enough for the children, and I thought Dolly'd like dressing-up her Emily.'

Farewells were said and kisses given. Still no words came from Dolly, overwhelmed with good fortune, but the ardour of her kisses was gratitude enough for the old lady.

Dolly carried the resplendent Emily all the way home, and Francis carried them both for the last part of the journey. Windows and roofs were turned to gold by the sinking sun. The drop of water in the white stone by the gate gleamed like a jewel. From the height of her father's comfortable shoulder Dolly looked down upon the rose-bush, its flowers as blood-red as Emily's new cloak.

The scent brought memories of the bean-flowers' fragrance and the smell of crushed grass in the summer meadow. The ox-eyed daisies, the red sorrel, the rose-bush, and the pansies nodding on her mother's bonnet, seemed to whirl together in a dazzling summer dance.

Dizzy with happiness, dazed with golden light, at last Dolly found her tongue.

'Lovely,' she sighed, and fell instantly asleep.

CHAPTER 5

Soon after that golden day, Dolly started school. Ada had been attending the church school at the northerly end of Caxley for over a year, so that the younger child had heard about teachers and classes, sums and slates, and marching to music.

It sounded attractive, and though she dreaded leaving her mother, yet the thought of Ada's company was supporting. She was, too, beginning to look for more than the little house and garden could provide in interest. Her mother was usually too busy to answer questions or to tell her stories. Her father was much more of a playmate, but he was seldom there. With Ada away at school young Dolly was restless, and when, at last, she was told that she would be accompanying Ada, the child's spirits rose.

She was dressed with particular care that first morning. Over her navy blue serge frock she wore a clean holland pinafore. With a thrill of pride she watched her mother pin a handkerchief to the pinafore, on the right side of her chest, conveniently placed for use in 'Handkerchief Drill Time' which, as Ada had explained frequently, came just before morning prayers and appeared to rank as rather more important. It made Dolly feel important, one of a fraternity, and she wore this emblem of enfranchisement with deep satisfaction.

Her mother sat her on the table to lace her little black boots and tie the strings of her bonnet. The red bobbles on the table-cloth joggled as she wriggled in excitement. Ada, already dressed, jumped up and down the path between the open front door and the gate, looking out for Esther, an older girl, who took her to and from school. This morning she wanted to tell Esther that her sister was coming, and her mother too, and that Esther need not wait for them.

Esther was a tall thin child, with a long pale face and prominent teeth. She looked perpetually frightened, as no doubt she was. Her father was a heavy drinker and violent in his cups. He was a ploughman, but at this time when so much arable land was being turned over to pasture, he had been put to sheep-minding, hedging and ditching, mucking out stables and cowsheds, and  other jobs which he considered beneath him. Had he realised it, he was fortunate to have been kept in work at all by his hard-pressed employer. With the influx of cheap grain from the United States and Canada, prices for English wheat had dropped so disastrously in the last few years that he, and many like him, had turned to grazing in the hope of recovery. That, too, was to prove a forlorn hope within a few years, as frozen meat from Australia and New Zealand, and dairy products from Denmark and Holland poured into the country. It was small wonder that men who had spent their lives on the land now uprooted themselves and took their strength and their diminishing hopes to the towns. Others, like Esther's father, too stupid to understand the significance of the catastrophe, either suffered in bewildered silence, watching their families sink and starve, or sought comfort in drink or the militant succour offered them by the evangelical churches.

Transition is always hazardous and distressing. The working people of rural England at that time were largely untaught and trusted the gentry's guidance. They witnessed the crumbling of a way of life, unchanged for centuries, and distress, resentment and fear harried the older generation. The younger people saw opportunities in towns or, better still, overseas, and thousands of them left the villages never to return. Little Dolly, kicking her legs on the table as they waited for Esther, was to be a mature woman before English farming found its strength again, and by that time machines would have come to take the place of the men who had left the fields for ever.

'We don't want you, Esther,' shouted Ada exuberantly from the gate, as the lanky child came into sight. Mary lifted Dolly hastily to the floor and hurried outside, much vexed.

'Ada! You rude little girl!' scolded her mother. 'You come in, my dear,' she added kindly to timid Esther, 'and take no notice of Ada.'

She picked up three small parcels, wrapped in white paper, and gave one to each child. Dolly and Ada knew that they contained a slice of bread spread with real lard from grandma's, and sprinkled with brown sugar.

'There's a stay-bit for you,' she said, 'to eat at playtime. Mind you don't lose it, and no eating it before then, or the teacher will give you the cane.'

Esther put hers carefully in the pocket of her shabby coat, but Ada thrust her own and Dolly's into a canvas satchel which had once been Francis's dinner bag, and now carried such provender, as well as books or a pencil, to school.

'Stay by the gate while I gets my bonnet,' said Mary, lifting her coat from a peg on the door and thrusting her arms into it. Her everyday bonnet was kept on a shelf just inside the cupboard under the stairs. She tied it on briskly. The only mirror downstairs was a broken triangle propped in the scullery window for Francis's shaving operations, and Mary did not bother to waste time in consulting this. She shifted a saucepan to the gentler heat at the side of the hob, locked the front door, took Dolly's hand, and hurried schoolward.

Ada and Esther went before them, the younger child skipping

cheerfully, swinging the satchel and quite unconcerned by her recent scolding. She was beginning to be bored by Esther's attentions. Strong and lusty, Ada could have done without Esther's support after the first week at school. Her boisterous good spirits disarmed any possible bullies, and her tough little fists would have attacked anyone foolish enough to molest her.

Esther adored her. To look after Ada made the pathetic child feel wanted and useful. Mary's bright smile and her occasional present of an apple or rough sandwich as 'a stay-bit' warmed Esther's heart. In the Clares' modest home Esther saw all that she wanted most. Mary knew this, and knew too that her young children were as safe in Esther's devoted care as they would be in her own.

Dolly's spirits were high too, as she struggled to keep up with the others. She could hear the school bell ringing in the distance, and looked forward to the delights of sitting in a desk and having a multitude of children for company. If Ada said school was fun, then it must be. For nearly five years Ada had told Dolly what to expect. So far she had never been wrong. Trustingly, she trotted behind Ada's prancing heels.

The bell had stopped ringing by the time they turned the corner and came in sight of the asphalt playground in front of the school. Children were forming lines, and two or three teachers stood in front of them. One had a whistle and blew it fiercely.

'Straighten up, Standard Four,' she shouted. 'Take distance, there. Take distance!'

The children lifted their arms to shoulder level and moved back to make a space. Dolly watched in amazement.

Her mother kissed her swiftly and put her hand in Ada's.

'You stay with Ada, my love, till your teacher fetches you. They knows all about you, 'cos I filled in the form the other day.'

Dolly's eyes began to fill with tears, and her mother dabbed them hastily with the corner of her scarf. Her voice grew urgent.

'There, there now! Don't 'ee cry. The others'll think you're a baby. I must be getting back to cook your dinner, my lovey, and Ada and Esther'll bring you home very soon.'

Wisely, she hurried away, doing her best to smile cheerfully at her woebegone little daughter, who looked smaller than ever against the bigger children ranked in the playground.

'Hurry up, you three!' called the teacher with the whistle, and Mary saw the three children scurry into place. With considerable relief she noticed that Dolly, though pale, was now dry-eyed. She turned towards home realising, with a shock, that she was alone for the first time for years, and that she would find her house empty.

Twenty minutes later Dolly sat in a long desk close beside Ada. There were four children on the narrow plank seat which they shared, and Dolly was perched precariously at the end, her boots swinging in mid-air.

Before each child was a fascinating square carved into the long desk top. Although Dolly did not know it then, she was soon to learn that each one measured a foot by a foot, and that the little squares inside were each a square inch. Under her lashes she looked to see if her companions were as interested in their property as she was, but they were old campaigners of several terms' standing, contemporaries of Ada's, and were sitting bolt upright with their arms folded tidily across their backs.

Dolly put out an exploratory finger and traced the lines lovingly.

'Don't fidget, dear,' said Miss Turner, briskly. 'Hands behind backs.'

Dolly attempted to put her hands away as neatly as her sister, but found the position extremely uncomfortable. However, Miss Turner seemed satisfied with the effort, and returned to her scrutiny of a large book on the desk before her, leaving Dolly free to gaze about her.

The schoolroom was long and contained three classes. All the children faced the same way, and all sat in desks holding four.

At Dolly's end of the room Miss Turner faced her two rows of infants. In the middle of the room sat the teacher who had wielded the whistle. Her name was Miss Broomhead, Dolly learnt later, and not unnaturally she possessed a multitude of nicknames, none of them flattering. The children in her class were aged from seven to ten or eleven, and their desks were a size larger than the infants', and had four inkwells spaced at regular intervals, whereas the infants' had none.

At the far end of the room the headmaster, Mr Bond, held sway. He was small and neat, with white hair, very blue eyes, and a sharp tongue. He was a stickler for punctuality, tidiness, cleanliness and obedience. Good work took its place after these four virtues. Very often, as he well knew, it followed automatically, for orderly habits make an orderly mind just as surely as an orderly mind expresses itself in a tidy manner. For the eager, clever child, however, whose mind outstripped his pen, Mr Bond's standards could be heart-breaking. He might do a dozen sums of horrid intricacy and get them all correct, but if one small blot or crossing out marred his page then Mr Bond's red pencil slashed across the whole, and he must perforce copy it all out again under threat of a caning. With the amazing patience and endurance of childhood, these conditions were accepted, and Mr Bond was not considered unreasonable in his demands. In fact, he was respected for his high standards, and in an age which was geared to great efforts for a small return, Mr Bond's methods, harsh as they might seem to later schoolmasters, suited his pupils and prepared them for sterner employers in the future.

Two great fireplaces stood at each end of the long wall facing the children. One stood conveniently near Mr Bond's desk, the other by Miss Turner's. Miss Broomhead, unluckily placed in the middle, had to be content with any ambience cast by a large photograph of Queen Victoria which held pride of place in the exact centre of the wall behind her. The Queen was in her widow's weeds, a small crown upon her head, and a veil flowing from it to her shoulders. One plump hand rested on an occasional table, and her gaze was fixed upon some unseen object which appeared to provide her with no satisfaction. Above the heavy frame were lodged two small Union Jacks thick with chalk dust from the blackboards and soot from the fires.

Directly beneath the Queen stood a glass case containing a stuffed fox against a background of papery ferns and tufts of wiry heather. His white teeth looked very sharp and his glass eyes very bright. Dolly wondered, in her innocence, if she would ever be allowed to play with him. At the infants' end, a smaller glass case held a stuffed red squirrel holding a hazel nut in its tiny claws; and at Mr Bond's end a sinister collection of common amphibians, including frogs and newts, at all stages of development, disported themselves among dead reeds and moulting bulrushes arranged around an improbable-looking painted pond.

Six brass oil lamps, with white shades which reminded Dolly of her father's summer thatching hat, hung from the lofty roof and swung very slowly when the door slammed. Three tall narrow windows, set very high in the wall at each end of the room, provided most of the daylight, but two smaller ones, behind the children, added their share, and a constant villainous draught for good measure. Children in the back desks, just below these windows, philosophically endured stiff necks and ear-ache, or used their wits to gain a move to a desk nearer the front.

Almost a hundred children were taught in this one room, and, as Dolly soon discovered, it was amazing how quietly the work was done. Heavy boots on bare boards made far more noise than the voices of teachers and pupils, and when, in the long sleepy afternoons, the bigger children were writing or reading silently to themselves, the atmosphere grew so soporific that many an infant, essaying a wobbly pot hook, let fall both slate pencil and slate, and fell asleep with its head pillowed on the carved square of the desk lid. When this happened, wise Miss Turner let sleeping babes lie, rousing them only when the clock said a quarter to four. Then, with bewildered eyes and one flushed cheek grotesquely marked with inch squares, they would return reluctantly to this world, submit dazedly to buttoning and tying, and so stumble away with big sisters to the haven of home.

School proved much more complex for Dolly than Ada had led her to believe. The parting from her mother affected the younger child severely, although she showed little, and departed docilely each morning holding Esther's hand. She had always been much more dependent on her mother than Ada, and once the older child had gone to school the bond between Mary and Dolly had been stronger than ever.

One incident about this time the child remembered all her life. She came upon her mother sitting by the window one day, holding a needle to the light. She frowned with intense concentration, trying to jab the cotton through the eye. Dolly spoke to her, but so intent was she upon the task in hand, that her mother made no sign, but simply bent closer to the window, her eyes glittering and fixed in awful absorption.

To Dolly the remembrance of her mother's complete mental withdrawal on that occasion was terrifying. Far easier to bear were her brief physical absences to the garden or to the rooms upstairs. But to be so close to one's mother, to put one's hand on her skirt, to speak to her and then to find she was not there, and that one was of no more significance than the wallpaper beside her, was an experience fraught with terror. It was also indicative, she realised later, of the deep need she had of her mother's affection.

But once she had made the daily parting and was on her way to school, Dolly, facing the inevitable, put her mother from her thoughts. Her new companions were overwhelming. Everything about them intrigued the little girl who had known only a few people until now.

In the first place there were so many of them, and they were so diverse. Her path did not cross those of the bigger children very often, but there was surprise and variety enough in the thirty or so boys and girls whose class she shared.

Much to her relief she was allowed to sit by Ada, but she had been moved to an inside position on the bench, and on her right hand side sat Maud and Edith. Edith at the end of the bench was a nondescript five-year-old, the child of a shopkeeper in the High Street. She was the sort of child who fades into the background of a class, having nothing outstanding to make her memorable. Her hair was mousy, her eyes hazel, her dress was drab but tidy. Quiet to the point of apathy, producing neat undistinguished work, dully obedient, Edith existed at the end of the bench.

But Maud was quite a different matter. To little Dolly, pressed so closely to her, Maud was as strange and foreign as a Chinaman. The first thing one noticed about her was her aroma. A sourish, slightly cheesy smell emanated from her, and this became overpowering when the four jumped to their feet, tipping up the long bench behind them, before marching out to play. This movement seemed to release a bouquet of scents from Maud's disturbed clothing, and added to the basic sourness there would be whiffs of stale frying, paraffin and vinegar. Later in life Dolly Clare recognised these mingled smells as the poignant scent of poverty.

Maud was very thin. She wore a tartan frock meant for someone much bigger and stouter. Her long pale neck, shadowy with grime, protruded like a stem from a flower pot, and the shock of red hair atop might have been mistaken for a shaggy bronze chrysanthemum. Her eyes were pale blue and protuberant, her wide mouth perpetually open, and she fidgeted and wriggled without ceasing, thus drawing upon herself a rattle of fire from Miss Turner's tongue.

'Sit still over there!' she would command, turning the frosty glare of her glasses upon Dolly's desk. Poor Dolly would flush pink with shame, but the guilty Maud would be unabashed, and giggle behind a dirty hand.

Maud's mottled mauve legs were bare, which slightly shocked Dolly in those days of muffled limbs. Her bony feet were thrust into a pair of broken boys' shoes, so ill-fitting that they frequently fell off, exposing Maud's claw-like toes. She was constantly hungry, and never owned a handkerchief. Light-witted (and light-fingered, too, it proved later), Maud was the pathetic product of one aspect of England's industrial prosperity. Her home was in the marsh.

Dolly grew very fond of her. Maud was loud in her praise of Dolly's clothes and her soft curls which she delighted in stroking. Her own rough thatch grew more tangled daily as she scratched her head remorselessly. Dolly accepted the scratching, the smell and the giggling of her neighbour without rancour, but wished she would not fidget so much and draw attention to the bench as a whole. Years later, when Dolly herself was a teacher, she wondered that Maud, and many others like her, had not fidgeted more, plagued as they were with the torments of the poor. Unwashed and tangled hair harboured head-lice, bodies packed four to a bed bred fleas, inadequate diet nourished thread-worms – but not their hosts. One stand-pipe of cold water, in a yard, to serve twelve houses, did not encourage cleanliness. Large families meant exhausted mothers, leading to neglect or despair. When you came to think of it, the grown-up Miss Clare mused, it was a tribute to Maud's resilience that she lived at all.

There was a number of children from the marsh in Dolly's class, and young as she was, she soon noticed that they incurred Miss Turner's wrath more frequently than the rest of the class. To Dolly's tender heart this seemed monstrously unfair, but in the nature of things this was understandable. Their work was as dirty and careless as their dress. They lacked concentration and energy. It is difficult to attend to abstract things when one is pinched with hunger in the middle and aflame with head-lice at one end and chilblains at the other. Miss Turner was not unsympathetic, but she had a job to do, and had to do it, moreover, under the eye of a vigilant headmaster.

Consequently, she berated the slow, whipped on the lazy with the lash of her tongue, and encouraged the zealous with hearty praise. She was a good teacher, brisk and cheerful, with a rough and ready way of dealing with the offenders, who seemed, to Dolly, almost always from 'the marsh lot'.

One incident, and its sequel, brought home to the little girl the shattering unpredictability of this new world of school. A squeal of pain from the boys' side of the class made them all look up from the pot hooks and hangers they were writing with their squeaky slate pencils. Miss Turner hurried forward to investigate.

'Miss,' whimpered one five-year-old, holding up a quivering forefinger, 'Fred Borden's been and bit me.'

Sure enough, the tell-tale teeth marks were still red upon the shaking finger, and Fred Borden was pink and sullen.

'Couldn't help it,' said the culprit unconvincingly. Miss Turner swept into action.

'By my desk,' she ordered, following the child to the front of the class.

'Put your slates down,' said Miss Turner, obviously enjoying the chance of a practical lesson in behaviour. 'Here's a little boy who likes to bite other people. Should boys bite?'

'No, miss,' came the self-righteous sing-song.

'Only dogs bite,' affirmed Miss Turner severely, turning to the shrinking malefactor. 'And as you seem to have turned into a dog this morning, I shall have to treat you like one.'

Dolly was appalled. Poor Fred! Did this mean he would be beaten? Dolly shook at the mere idea. He looked so sad, and no bigger than herself, that her gentle heart throbbed with pain for him.

Miss Turner bustled to a cupboard and returned with a length of tape. She tied one end loosely round the child's neck, and there was a titter of laughter which grew to a great shout as she motioned to the child to crouch on all fours as she tied the other end to the leg of the desk.

'There, now,' said Miss Turner, red with bending and the success of her lesson. 'You must stay tied up until dinner time. We can't have dangerous animals that bite running loose in the classroom, can we, children?'

'No, miss,' chanted the class smugly.

'Back to work, then,' commanded Miss Turner, resuming her patrolling up and down the aisles. Dolly took up her slate pencil with a shaking hand.

That anyone – especially someone grown-up – could tie up

another person like an animal horrified the child. To be sure, Fred Borden, who had feared a trip to the other end of the room where the cane lay on Mr Bond's desk, seemed quite cheerful as he sat on the floor by the desk. But Dolly, putting herself in his place, would have been prostrate with shame. To have sat there, publicly humiliated, enduring the gaze of thirty heartless school-fellows, would have broken Dolly. In fact, Fred Borden was enjoying the limelight, felt no hardship in missing a writing lesson, and considerable relief at getting off so lightly.

At twelve o'clock he was released, and the children trooped home to dinner. It so happened that Fred Borden and another boy were dawdling along the road as Esther, Ada and Dolly came up to them. The boys turned and spread their arms out to bar the way. They both grinned cheerfully. They felt no malice – this was just a reflex action when they saw three little girls trying to get by.

Esther stopped nervously, too frightened to protest, and near to tears. She lived considerably further than her charges, and time was short. She dreaded being late back to school.

Dolly, still shocked by the morning's experience, felt that she must tell poor Fred of her sympathy, but could not think how to begin.

At that moment, Ada went into action.

'Bow-wow! Who's a dog? Who bites? Who's a dog?' chanted Ada mockingly.

Fury at her sister's cruelty shook the words from Dolly's tongue. She stepped forward and put one small hand on Fred's filthy jersey. Her earnest face was very close to his.

'I was *sorry*,' she babbled incoherently. 'I was *sorry* she tied you up. She shouldn't have done that. I was *sorry*!'

To her amazement, Fred's grin vanished, and a menacing scowl took its place.

'Shut up, soppy!' he growled fiercely, and with venom he thrust the little girl away so forcefully that she fell backwards into Esther. Fist still raised, Fred followed her.

'What d'you want to hurt her for?' shrilled Esther, finding her voice.

'Because I 'ates 'er!' shouted Fred passionately. 'Because I 'ates all of you! You stuck-up lot!'

And with the hot tears springing to his eyes, he turned and fled down the narrow alley that led to the marsh.

CHAPTER 6

ONE windy March day in 1894 Francis Clare came home from work in a state of high excitement. He blew into the little living-room on a gust of wind that lifted the curtains and caused the fire to belch smoke.

'Well, Mary,' he cried, dropping his dinner satchel triumphantly on the table, 'I've got a house.'

'Francis! No! You mean it?'

'Sure as I'm here.'

'Where?'

'Beech Green.'

'But you've never been to Beech Green today?' queried Mary, still bewildered. The two little girls, playing with Emily on the rag hearthrug, gazed up at him as open-mouthed as their mother.

'No, no. I've been at Springbourne all day, like I said, thatching Jesse Miller's cow shed. He come up while I was working and says: "You the young fellow as near killed 'isself a year or two back and had a ride home in my cart?"'

'I told him I was. He's getting forgetful-like now he's old –
kept calling me by my father's name, but it appears one of his
chaps told him we was looking for a cottage, and he's got an
empty one we can have.

' "'Tisn't a palace," he said, "two up and two down, but a
pump inside and good cupboards. Take a look at it, and tell me
what you think. Two shillings a week rent old Bob used to
pay me before he left me to go to work in Caxley. That suits
me if it suits you." And he threw the key up to me, and off he
goes.'

'Well!' said Mary, flabbergasted. 'And what's it like?'

'Nice little place. Next door to Hundred Acre Field. Good
bit of garden and handy for the school. I reckon you'll like it.
We'll go over Sunday and you shall see it. Ma'll have the girls,
I don't doubt, and we can walk it easy in just over an hour.'

It was the most amazing news, and the family could hardly
eat for excitement. By the next Sunday, when Mary had seen
it and pronounced it perfect, all that remained to be done was
to give a week's notice to their landlord and accept Jesse Miller's
offer of a cart to carry the furniture from the Caxley home to
the new one.

They were to move on Lady Day, which gave them about
a fortnight in which to attend to the multitude of domestic
details involved in moving house. For the last few days the
Caxley home was almost unrecognisable. Curtains had been
taken down, cupboards cleared, boxes stood, roped and massive, in the most awkward places, and chaos reigned.

But for all the bustle and confusion, Mary and Francis smiled.
At last, they were leaving Caxley. At last, they were on their
way to the open country where their hearts had always been.

Hearing their mother sing, as she washed china and stored it
in a box stuffed with their father's thatching straw, the two
little girls exchanged secret smiles. Beech Green might be un-

known to them, but obviously there was no need for apprehension. Beech Green, it seemed, was the Promised Land.

The day of the move dawned still and cloudless. The Clare family was up betimes and the front door was propped open so that the coming of the farm cart could be instantly seen.

Breakfast was a picnic meal that day, of bread and cold bacon cut into neat cubes placed on a meat dish on the bare table, for such refinements as cooking pots, plates and table-cloths were all packed up.

It had been arranged that Mary and the children should travel on the cart with the furniture, while Francis stayed behind to lock up and return the key to the landlord.

'Jim's going to give us a hand putting our traps in at Beech Green,' said Francis, naming the carter who was to transport them, 'and I should be with you soon after you gets there. We'll be straight afore dark, my love, curtains up and all, you'll see.'

Outside, the early sunshine lit the tiny garden and shone through the open door upon the bare wall of the living-room. Perched on the budding rose bush, a speckled thrush sang his heart out, as if in farewell. It was strange, thought Mary suddenly, that she felt no pangs at parting from this her first home. Here the two babies had been born, and she and Francis had known happiness and misfortune. She had come across that uneven threshold as a bride, and was to leave as a wife and mother, but despite its associations, the house meant little to her. She would be glad to leave it.

There was a distant rumbling, which grew as they listened. Then came the sound of heavy hooves, and Jim's voice.

'Whoa there, old gal. Whoa, Bella!'

'He's come!' squeaked the two little girls, flying to the gate. The adventure had begun.

For the next hour or two Francis and Mary went back and forth from the house to the farm cart, helped by Jim who was almost as strong as the massive mare between the shafts. The children tore up and down in a state of wild excitement, getting in everyone's way, until Francis could stand it no longer.

'You two keep out o' this,' he said firmly. 'Play out the back or upstairs where we've done. We'll all be wore out before we starts.'

Ada skipped out through the back door, but Dolly made her way up the echoing shaky stairs to her empty bedroom. It was queer to see its bareness. There were dusky lines along the walls where the bed, the chest of drawers, and the cane-bottomed chair had stood. A blue bead glinted in a crack between two floor boards, and Dolly squatted down to prize it out.

Near her, where the skirting board joined the floor, was a small jagged hole where a mouse lived. Her mother had set a trap many times, but no mouse was ever caught. Dolly sometimes wondered if this were in answer to her fervent, but silent, prayers on these occasions. Each night, kneeling on the hard floor with her face muffled in the side of the white counterpane, she had chanted:

God bless Mummy,
God bless Daddy,
Aunties and Uncles,
And all kind friends,
And make me a GOOD girl,
For Jesus Christ's sake
Amen.

On the nights when the trap was set, she added fiercely and silently:

'And PLEASE DON'T let the mouse get caught,' before leaping into bed beside Ada, and drawing up the clothes.

Now, she thought, the mouse could have the whole house to live in, and would never see a trap again.

She wandered to the window and looked out into the back garden. Ada was trying to stand on her hands, supporting her legs against the fence. It was strange to think she would never do that again here. Dolly turned to look at the room again. It seemed to be waiting, it was so quiet and eerie. She felt as if she were intruding, as if the place she stood in were no longer hers.

Soon she heard her parents calling.

'Come on, Ada and Dolly! It's all ready now. Let's get you dressed.'

Within half an hour they were off.

Nearly seventy years later, the details of that amazing journey still remained clear in Miss Clare's memory. There had been an iron step, she remembered, to climb on in order to get into the cart. It was shiny with a hundred boot-scrapings, and had a crescent-shaped hole in it through which one had a terrifying glimpse of the road below.

Jim, Mary and the two children squeezed together on the plank seat that ran across the cart. Dolly felt most unsafe, for her feet would not reach the floor. Emily was tucked by her, but Jim said she had better be put in the back.

'Ain't no room for us to breathe, let alone your dolly,' said Jim cheerfully. 'Give 'er 'ere.'

He clambered down again and Dolly reluctantly handed Emily, in her red cape, into his huge knobbly hand. He went to the rear of the cart and propped Emily up in a chair.

'There she be,' called Jim. 'Now 'er's got a clear view of the road.'

Satisfied, Dolly settled down to present delights. The horse's massive brown haunches, moving just below her, fascinated the child. Leather squeaked, brass jingled, wooden wheels rumbled, and the whole cart seemed alive with movement and noises.

A gentle climb, from the river valley where Caxley lay, occupied the first mile or so of the journey. The sun was high now, and from her lofty seat Dolly could see over the hedges into the meadows. They steamed gently in the growing heat, for they were wet from overnight rain.

About half a mile before it entered the village of Beech Green the road plunged down a short steep hill between high banks topped with massive beech trees. It was the first time that the child had seen great roots writhing out of the soil like underground branches. It seemed to make this new world even more strange and foreign.

'Nearly there,' said her mother, putting a steadying arm round Dolly, so that she did not slide forward on to Belle's great back. 'You'll see your new home soon.'

They emerged from the tunnel of trees and began to rumble through the scattered village. Ada noticed the school standing back from the road. A few children, playing in the dinner hour, watched their progress, and one child waved. Ada waved back energetically, but Dolly was too timid.

Their own house lay half a mile or so further, on the outskirts of Beech Green. Three miles further still lay the village of Fairacre where so much of little Dolly's life was to be spent.

Dolly's spirits rose with every turn of the wheel that took her further from Caxley. The light breeze stirred her hair, hanging now, almost to her shoulders, in blessed holiday freedom. The inevitable had happened at the Caxley school. The propinquity of Maud's auburn tangles had soon led to Dolly's head scratching, her mother's shocked discoveries, and the tight tying-back of poor Dolly's locks on school days. The feeling of wind in her hair enhanced the delights of the day as the child kept a look-out for the new cottage.

At last a bend in the road revealed it – a snug, thatched, tight little beauty of a house, set behind a thick hedge just quickening to green. The cart slurred to a stop, the noises ceased, and the full quiet harmony of the wide countryside became apparent.

Jim lifted the two children down. He and Mary began to busy themselves with the load, helped by the vociferous Ada. Dolly, as if in a trance, pushed open the small gate and wandered past the cottage to the end of the garden. She had never realised that the world was so big.

Before her, beyond the garden hedge, sloped the gentle flanks of the downs with Hundred Acre Field at the base, and their tops, hazy in the distance, fading into the blue of the sky. Birds sang in the hedges, in the trees, and far above her in the blue and white sky. The happiness which had warmed Dolly in the flower-lit meadow on her way to her grandmother's returned to her with renewed strength.

She felt as a minnow, long held captive in a jam jar, must feel on being released into a brook; or as a bird set free from a cage into the limitless air. This was her element. These crisscross currents of scent-laden air, spangled with bird-song, splashed with sunshine, flowed around her, lifting her spirits and quickening her senses.

Dolly Clare had come home.

Now, a lifetime later, white-haired Miss Clare stood in the same garden, gazing at the same view and drawing from it the same comfort and strength which it had always given. Her hands were full of roses. Some would stand in the small sitting room, but the choicest would be put beside Emily Davis's bed in the spare bedroom.

The thought of Emily reminded Miss Clare again of the lost doll. It was dusk, she recalled, before the first Emily had been missed. Distressed though she was, little Dolly had been less upset than her parents feared, for the enchantment of the day still possessed her.

'I'll see Jim tomorrow,' promised Francis. 'He'll have her safe, never fear.'

But Emily was not with Jim. She had fallen from the back of the cart and lay face downward at the side of the lane between Caxley and Beech Green. A ten-year-old boy, who had spent the morning rattling two stones in a tin to scare the birds from his master's crop, found her as he went home to dinner. He turned her over with the broken toe-cap of his boot, and snorted with scorn.

'Some kid's old dolly!' he shouted to the wind, and booted it, in a magnificent arc, over the hedge.

It was a week before she was found, and Dolly had shed many tears of mourning. A man, cutting back the hedge, had discovered the sodden doll and taken it to the local shop, where Francis later collected it.

'There, my dear,' he said to Dolly, 'now you can be happy again.'

Dolly took the long-lost doll into her arms, but never completely into her heart again.

Emily looked so different. She had the pale remote air of one who has been ill for a long time. One eye had gone, and though Mary sewed two white linen shirt buttons in place of her former eyes, this only added to the strangeness of the doll in her young mistress's eyes. She cared for her as zealously as she had always done, putting her to bed, tying on the red cloak before taking her into the garden, and propping a cushion behind her back when she sat at table. But the glory was gone.

It may have been that the new living Emily had taken her place. Certainly she had become very dear to young Dolly.

'And still is,' said old Miss Clare, stirring herself from her reminiscences.

The clock struck twelve inside the house, and from the distant village school Miss Clare heard the shouts of children released from bondage.

'I've done nothing but day-dream,' Miss Clare told herself, returning from the noonday blaze to the shade of the kitchen. 'Emily will be here before I'm ready for her. But then that's one of the pleasures of growing old,' she comforted herself.

Singing softly, roses in hand, she mounted the stairs to the waiting room.

PART TWO *Beech Green*

CHAPTER 7

LIFE at Beech Green was an exhilarating affair, after the confines of Caxley, and made all the richer by the friendship with Emily Davis.

She was a mischievous, high-spirited child, the middle one of seven children. All nine of the Davises lived, as snug and gay as a nestful of wrens, in a tiny cottage at the end of a row of four.

Dolly found her way there before she had lived a week at her new home. There was a happy-go-lucky atmosphere about the Davises' house which enchanted the little girl who had been more primly brought up. She tumbled in and out of their home, revelling in the games, the nonsense and the carefree coming and going of the seven children and their numerous friends.

Emily's father was a gardener at the manor house at Beech Green. He was a giant of a man, with a face as brown and wrinkled as a walnut. Two bright blue eyes blazed from his weatherbeaten countenance, and his laugh shook the cottage. 'My husband's a very larky man,' Mrs Davis would say proudly. 'Likes his joke, and that.'

She was barely five feet high, with a figure so neat and child-like that it seemed impossible that she could be the mother of such a large and boisterous brood. Her energy was boundless. She scrubbed and polished the little house, cooked massive meals, washed mountains of linen, and then knitted and sewed, or tended her flower garden, as a relaxation. Throughout it all she laughed and sang, finding time to play with her children, cuffing them good-naturedly when they needed correction, and seeming, at the end of the day, to be as fresh as when she rose at five-thirty.

Dolly loved Mrs Davis dearly. Her warm and casual friendliness made her feel part of the family, and her self-assurance grew.

In the corner of the cottage living-room sat old Mr Davis, Emily's grandfather. He had been a carter, but now, unable to work regularly, he made a few pence by mending pots and pans for the neighbours. His right hand was encased in a black kid glove, which fascinated young Dolly.

One day, soon after her arrival at Beech Green, the old man caught the child's eyes fixed upon his hand. A soldering iron was heating in the open fire, and between his knees old Mr Davis held an upturned kettle.

'You be wondering why I keeps me glove on, I'll wager,' he grunted.

Dolly smiled shyly.

'Well, I ain't agoing to take it off to show you, me little maid, or you'd 'ave a fright. I ain't got much of me fingers left, if the truth be told.'

He bent forward, breathless with the effort, and removed the red-hot iron from the fire. Dolly, with a thrill of horror, saw how he held it gripped in the palm of his hand. He dipped the iron in a little tin on the fender, and a hot pungent smoke rose from the sizzling liquid.

'I was out in that ol' snowstorm for two days,' said the old man. 'Afore you was born or thought of, that was. In 1881 – getting on for fourteen year ago. I'd taken a load of hay over to Springbourne that day, and it was snowing pretty lively as I went. But how the Hanover I got back as fur as I did that afternoon, I never could tell. Just this side of the downs I 'ad to give in. I cut the horses loose and said: "Git on 'ome, you two, while you can." I felt fair lonely watching them slipping and sliding down the hill, up to their bellies in snow, leaving me on me own.'

'You should have sat on one,' said Dolly gravely.

'Easier said than done,' grunted Mr Davis, applying his soldering iron to the kettle. There was silence while he surveyed his handiwork for a minute or two, and then he resumed.

'The snow was that thick, and swirling around so, them two horses vanished pretty quick. I could 'ear 'em snorting with fright and shaking their heads. They 'adn't seen nothing like it, you see. Nor me, for that matter.

'There I was, and I couldn't make up me mind to stop in the cart or try and plod on home and risk it.'

'What did you do?' asked Dolly.

'Risked it,' said the old man laconically. 'Risked it, and fell in a dam' ditch I never knew was there, and 'ad to stop there two days. I ain't seen nothing like that blizzard before or since. If it 'adn't a been for the two horses getting back I reckon I'd a been there still. They never got home till next day, and it took four chaps searching in turn to find me, it was that cruel.'

'Did you shout?' asked Dolly.

'I was past shouting after the first 'alf-hour,' answered Mr Davis, holding the kettle to the light and squinting inside it. 'By the time they dug me out I was as stiff as this 'ere iron. Stayed in bed a week, I did, and 'ad to 'ave three fingers and two toes plucked orf. The frost-bite, you see.'

Dolly nodded, appalled.

'I shan't forget 1881 in a 'urry,' said the old man, and thrust the soldering iron back into the red heart of the coals with a deft thrust of his maimed hand.

*   *   *

The Davises were not the only new friends. Francis and Mary Clare blossomed in their country surroundings, and the neighbourliness which they had missed so sorely in Caxley now seemed doubly dear.

The family had for so long been thrust in upon itself. The next door neighbours at Caxley, cross and aged, had been ever present in Mary's thoughts, and Dolly and Ada were often scolded for making a noise that might penetrate the thin dividing wall. Fear of strangers, and particularly of 'the marsh lot', kept country-bred Mary from making many friends in Caxley. Francis's illness and their pinching poverty were other factors in 'keeping themselves to themselves'.

Back in the country again, fellows of a small community, Mary and Francis felt their tension relax. A move is always an excitement in a village, and by the end of the first long day the family had met more than a dozen neighbours, some prompted by kindness, some by curiosity, who had called to welcome them.

Within a few weeks Francis had the cottage garden dug and planted, and found he had already promised to exhibit something in the local autumn flower show which was to be held at Fairacre. Mary, to her surprise, found that she had been persuaded to join the Glee Club, run on Friday nights by the redoubtable Mr Finch in his schoolroom.

'Us makes our own fun,' Mrs Davis said to Mary. ''Tis all very fine for the gentry to go to Caxley in their carriages for a ball at the Corn Exchange, but us ordinary folk, as goes on Shanks's pony, gets our fun in the village.'

And Mary, with her two little girls safely at school all day, and a husband back at work, was only too ready to join in the simple homely fun of which she had been starved for so long.

Dolly and Ada took to the village school like ducks to water. They had been well drilled at Caxley and found that the work here was well within their grasp. Their classmates were some-what impressed by the two new girls who had experienced the superior instruction of a town school, and Dolly and Ada felt pleasantly distinguished.

The smaller numbers made school life much less frightening for timid Dolly, and gave Ada greater scope for her powers of leadership. In no time she was the acknowledged queen of the playground, and had all the younger children vying for her favours, and the thrill of 'playing with Ada'. Mr Finch, who hid a genuine fondness for children beneath his pompous veneer, was glad to have such a bright pupil among his scholars, and Mrs Finch, who had some difficulty with discipline, was relieved to find that Dolly was as sedate as she was hard-working.

But the greatest joy for Dolly in this happy new life was the discovery of the infinite beauties in the natural world about her. That first glimpse of Beech Green and the realisation that she had found her real home, was repeated daily in a hundred different ways. The walk to school took about a quarter of an hour, and revealed dozens of enchanting things.

In that first spring, Dolly discovered that a bed of white violets grew on the left-hand bank just before the farm gate. They were well hidden by fine dry grass, but their heady scent betrayed them, and the child exulted in the pure whiteness, enhanced by the spot of yellow stamens lurking in its depths, of each small flower. Almost opposite grew a rarer type of violet, almost pink in colour, which was much sought after by the little girls of Beech Green. Dolly soon grew wise enough to keep the news of its flowering to herself.

Nearer the school, the lane was shaded by elm trees which grew upon steep banks. Here Dolly found a pink and fleshy plant, which Mr Finch told her was toothwort. It was un-attractive, and reminded Dolly of the pink pendulous sows in the farmyard as they lumbered about among their squealing young. But it had its fascination for the town-bred child, and she felt proud to see it put on the window-sill at school, neatly labelled by Mr Finch's own pen.

There were terrifying things too to encounter on the walk to school. Behind the farm gate, just beyond the violet bed, a dozen grey and white geese honked and hissed, stretching sinuous waving necks, and menacing the child with their icy blue eyes and cruel orange bills. Dolly shouted as bravely as the other children when the geese were safely barred, but sometimes the gate was open, and the geese paraded triumphantly up and down the lane. Then Dolly would scramble up the steep bank, over the roots of the elm trees and the tooth-wort, and try to gain the safety of the cornfield beyond, while the geese stretched their great wings and ran, hideously fast, creating a clamour that could be heard a mile away.

The geese were frightening enough, but even more disconcerting was Mabel, who lived in a cottage half way to school. She was a grotesque, misshapen figure, almost as broad as she was tall, the victim of some glandular disease which was incurable at that time. Mentally she was aged about six, although she had been born thirty years earlier, and she played with a magnificent doll all day long. In the winter Mabel was invisible to Beech Green, for she was closely, and lovingly, confined in the stuffy little house by her doting parents. But during the warm weather the pathetic stumpy figure sat in a basket chair placed on the front path. From there she watched the neighbours go by as she nursed the expensive doll.

'Them poor Bells,' the villagers said, with genuine sympathy, "as got enough to drive them silly theirselves with that Mabel. Got to be watched every minute of the day! But don't 'er mother keep 'er beautiful?'

Cleanliness was a much-prized virtue in Beech Green, and Mabel was held up as a shining example of Mrs Bell's industry. The poor idiot was always clothed in good quality dresses, covered with a snowy starched and goffered pinafore. Her coarse scanty hair, as bristly as that which grew upon the pigs' backs in the farmyard nearby, was tied back with a beautiful satin ribbon. Her podgy yellow face, from which two dark eyes glinted from slanting slits, was shiny with soap, and her fat little legs were always encased in the finest black stockings, with never so much as a pinpoint of a hole in sight.

To Dolly's terror, Mabel took an instant liking to her, and would waddle to the gate, holding up the doll and uttering thick guttural cries of pleasure. Dolly's first impulse was to run away, but her mother had spoken to her firmly.

'You can thank your stars you weren't born like Mabel, and just you be extra kind to that poor child – for child she is, for all her thirty years. No flinching now, if she comes up to you, and you let her touch you too, if she's a mind to! She's as gentle as a lamb, and the Bells have enough to put up with without people giving their only one the cold shoulder!'

And so Dolly steeled herself to smile upon the squat unlovely figure behind the cottage gate, and sometimes put a violet or two into that thick clumsy hand, and admired the doll with sincerity. She never saw Mabel outside the house or the garden, and never understood one word that fell from those thick lips; but when, in three or four years' time, the child mercifully died, she missed her sorely, and could only guess at the loss suffered by Mr Bell, and still more by Mrs Bell, whose clothes line had fluttered daily with the brave array of Mabel's finery.

Looking back later, to those early days at Beech Green, Miss Clare was amazed to think how many subnormal and eccentric people there were among that small number in those late Victorian days. There were many reasons. Inbreeding was a common cause, for lack of transport meant that the boys and girls of the village tended to marry each other, and the few families there became intricately related. Lack of skilled medical attention, particularly during childbirth, accounted for some deformities of mind and body, and the dread of mental hospitals – sadly justified in many cases – kept others from seeking help with their problems. Certainly, when Dolly first went to live at Beech Green, there were half a dozen souls in the neighbourhood who were as much in need of attention as poor Mabel.

There was the boy who had epileptic fits, who sat in the desk next to Ada, and was looked upon with more affection than distress by his classmates, as the means of enlivening Mr Finch's boring lessons. There was old Mrs Marble, who gibbered and shook her fist at the children from the broken window of her filthy cottage near the school, and who would certainly have been ducked in the horsepond had she had the misfortune to have been born a century earlier. There was a very nasty man who delighted in walking about the woods and lanes with his trousers over his arm, frightening the women and little girls out of their wits, but excused by the men as 'only happening when the moon was at the full, poor fellow.'

Then there were the three White children, abysmally slow at lessons, but with tempers of such uncontrollable violence that the whole school went in terror of them. How much of this vicious frenzy was due to mental disorder, and how much to their parents' treatment of it, was debatable. It was the custom of Mr and Mrs White to lock their refractory offspring in a cupboard under the stairs where, in the smelly darkness among the old shoes and coats that hung there, they were allowed to scream, sob, fight, pummel the door, and exhaust their hysteria before being let out again, some hours later, white and wild-eyed and ready to fall into their nightmare-haunted beds.

Even the great ones of the village had their sufferings. The lady of the manor, Mrs Evans, whose visits to the school meant much curtseying and bobbing, had one frail chick among her six sturdy ones, and Miss Lilian was never seen without a maid or her governess in attendance ready to direct her charge's wan looks towards anything of cheer.

As young Dolly soon discovered, Beech Green had its darker side, the reverse of the bright flower-decked face which charmed the newcomers. But it all added to the excitement of daily living. It gave the solemn little girl a chance to observe human frailties and quirks of behaviour, and gave her too an insight into the courage and good humour with which her fellows faced personal tragedy.

These early lessons were to stand her in good stead, for before long she too would be involved in a family disaster whose repercussions were to echo down many years of her adult life.

In welcoming all that life in Beech Green offered her, in both happiness and horror, the child unwittingly prepared herself for the testing time which lay ahead.

CHAPTER 8

THE first intimation of the event which was to colour so many years of Dolly Clare's later life was her mother's visit to the doctor in May 1896.

Mary Clare suspected that she was pregnant again, and she viewed the situation with mixed feelings.

'Just got my two off to school,' she confided resignedly to Mrs Davis one morning, 'and then another turns up. All that washing again, and bad nights, and mixing up feeding bottles! Somehow I don't take to the idea like I did, but Francis is that pleased I haven't the heart to tell him it's not all honey for me.'

'You waits till you has seven,' commented Mrs Davis cheerfully. 'Time enough to gloom then, I can tell you. Why, your two girls can give you a hand, and if it's a boy you'll be looked after proper in your old age!'

Somewhat comforted, Mary Clare made her way, one Tuesday morning, to the converted stable in the manor grounds where Dr Fisher held his weekly surgery.

'There's plenty to be thankful for,' she told herself, as she trudged up the broad drive between the flowering chestnut trees. 'Francis is as pleased as Punch, and he's in work again. And this place is far better to have a baby in than that Caxley hovel. It can lie in the garden, and I'll get the washing dry lovely with the winds we get here. And Mrs Davis is quite right about Dolly and Ada. They're big enough to help now they're eleven and nine.'

Her usual good spirits asserted themselves, and by the time the doctor had confirmed her suspicions she was facing the future with more hope. It is always heartening to be an object of interest, and Mary looked forward to many a cosy chat with her new neighbours, as she returned to her cottage.

Francis was jubilant when she told him that evening.

'It'll be a boy this time,' he assured her. 'You'll see, my love. A real fine son to carry on the thatching trade. The girls will be glad to hear the news.'

'They'll not learn it from me for a few months yet,' replied Mary tartly. 'Time enough for them to know when I takes to my bed.'

'If you don't want them to hear it from all the old gossips in the village,' warned her husband, 'you'd best tell 'em yourself before long.'

'Well, we'll see,' said Mary, more gently, recognising the wisdom of her husband's remark.

The baby was due in November, and the little girls were told one mellow September evening as they went to bed. Mary found it an embarrassing occasion and had steeled herself to it all day. She had rehearsed her short speech a dozen times, and delivered it with a beating heart and a pink face.

'I got something nice to tell you two, my dears. A wonderful secret. God's sending you a little brother next November,' she said, with rare piety.

At last it was out, and she waited, breathless, for the reaction.

Dolly sat up in bed, open-mouthed but silent. Ada bounced unconcernedly on to one side and said nonchalantly:

'Oh, I know! Jimmy Davis told me you was in kitten last June.'

Mary's pink face grew crimson with fury.

'The rude little boy!' she exclaimed, outraged. 'I'll see his mother hears of this, and gives him a good box side the ear, too! And I don't know as you don't deserve one, too, for listening to such rudeness!'

Seething with righteous indignation, Mary left her daughters unkissed, and slammed the door upon them. Relating it later to Francis she found her annoyance giving way to amusement as he gave way to his mirth.

'Looks to me quite simple,' laughed Francis. 'You wrapped it up too pretty, and Jimmy Davis put it real ugly, but one way or another, now they know. You go up and say good night to 'em and see how pleased they'll be.'

By the time darkness fell, peace was made, and the thought of a fifth member of the Clare family brought much joy to the four already awaiting him.

Amazingly, it was a boy. Mary's labour was grievously protracted, and the local midwife had been obliged to send for the doctor after hours of effort. Dolly and Ada had spent the night with the Davis household. Somehow two extra children fitted into the nutshell of a house with no difficulty, and they were thrilled to have a mattress on the floor of the girls' bedroom.

At dinner time next day they were told that a brother had arrived and they could go and see him.

'But mind you're quiet,' warned Mrs Davis. 'Your ma had a bad time with him and wants a good sleep.'

They rushed homeward, and the midwife led them on tiptoe to their parents' bedroom.

Pale, and appallingly tired, Mary smiled faintly at them from the pillows. Beside her lay a white bundle, containing what looked like a coconut from the Michaelmas fair. On closer inspection, Dolly could see the dark crumpled countenance of her brother, topped by a crop of black thatch. His eyes were glued together into thin slits, as though nothing in the world should prize him from the sleep that enfolded him.

Dolly was seriously disappointed. She had imagined someone looking like Mabel's beautiful doll, very small but exquisite. But she sensed that this was no time to express her dissatisfaction, and smiled as bravely as she could at her mother before taking Ada's hand and making her way to the door. Before she put her hand on the knob she noticed that her mother had fallen asleep again, with the same desperate concentration as the baby beside her.

That evening the two little girls returned to sleep at their own home. As soon as Francis came in he kissed them heartily, looking younger and more handsome than he had for many a year.

'Ain't he a lovely boy then?' he said to them proudly. 'Ain't you two lucky ones, having a brother after all?'

He led the way upstairs, and Francis bent over Mary and the baby. Mary looked less deathly pale, and smiled at the family, but the baby still slept, snuffling slightly in his shawl.

'You're all over bits,' Mary admonished her husband, as pieces of chaff fluttered down upon the bed from his working clothes. He laughed, and plucked a long golden straw that had lodged in the leather strap around his trouser leg.

'There you are, son,' he said, threading the bright strand through his child's small fingers. 'Get the feel of straw in your hand, and you'll grow up to be the best thatcher in England.'

It was that small incident that gave young Dolly a glimpse of her father's exultant pride, not only in his son, but in his work, and the new hope he now had of an assured future.

The baby thrived and was whole-heartedly adored by the family and the neighbours. His most fervent admirer was Emily Davis. One might have thought that the child had seen enough of babies, but little Frank Clare seemed dearer to Emily than her own young brothers, and she pushed his wicker pram as frequently as his sisters did.

By the time he was sitting up and taking notice of the world around him, the summer of 1897 had come and Beech Green was busy with preparations for the Diamond Jubilee of the aged Queen Victoria.

The local lord of the manor, Mr Evans, had invited everyone to games and a mammoth tea party, and excitement ran high as the great day in June approached. Many people remembered the celebrations ten years before when the sun had blazed upon a nation rejoicing in a reign of fifty years. This time, they said, it would be better still.

In the great world beyond Beech Green there was perhaps not quite the same fervour for the military pomp and processions as there had been at the Golden Jubilee. Many thinking men felt a growing distaste for imperialism, and distrusted 'jingoism', which they suspected inflamed a love of conquest for its own sake. This did not lessen the devotion to the Queen, who by now was an object of veneration to all her subjects. The majority of her countrymen had never known another monarch on the throne, and as the day of the Diamond Jubilee grew nearer, many tales were told of memorable events in her incredibly long reign.

Dolly's grandfather, on one of his visits to see the new baby, brought the remote figure of the great Queen very clearly to the child's mind.

'I was down at Portsmouth once, staying with my brother. August, it was, in the year 1875, and the royal yacht *Alberta* come over from Osborne one day. The Queen herself was aboard, and there was a shocking thing happened. Somehow or other a little yacht got across the *Alberta's* path and was run down. It sank in no time, and three poor souls was drownded. They told us the Queen was beside herself with distress, pacing up and down in the *Alberta* with the tears falling. Poor lady, she had a wonderful kind heart, and that were a sore and terrible grief to her.'

He presented the little girls with a Union Jack made by their grandmother so that they could hang it from the porch on Jubilee Day. On this occasion he had not brought his wife, for he had pedalled over on his old penny-farthing cycle, an archaic vehicle to which he was much attached. Dolly and Ada

watched him remount after tea, and waved the flag vigorously after his retreating figure.

The day itself dawned clear and shining. 'Real Queen's weather again,' people cried to each other as they bustled about. Household chores were done quickly that day to leave time for the preparations for the afternoon fun. In the grounds at the manor long trestle tables were spread with new lengths of unbleached calico for tablecloths, and on these were dozens of dishes of buns and lardy cakes, sandwiches and pies. Maids fluttered back and forth from the house bearing great trays of cups and saucers, tea urns, jugs, spoons and all the paraphernalia of rural junketings.

Dolly and Ada were beside themselves with excitement. All the schools had a holiday, and it was a thrill to wear one's best white frock with one's best black stockings and nailed boots. Their pink and blue sashes were freshly pressed, and Mary had tied hair ribbons to match upon her daughters' curls.

Dolly felt very sorry for one family who sat opposite her at the long tea table. They had recently lost their mother, and all the four children, even the youngest who could scarcely toddle, were clad in deepest black. From the crêpe bows which decorated their black hats to the toecaps of their heavy boots the gloom was unrelieved. Even their hands were encased in black cotton gloves which they did not remove even when eating. Under the brilliant blue sky, among the laughter and sunshine, they perched like four little black crows in a row, silent, and suffering the heat in stolid endurance.

After a colossal tea, one of the daughters of the house sang patriotic songs, accompanied by her sister, at the piano which had been wheeled out upon the grass from the drawing-room. Applause was polite but not very enthusiastic, and everyone, including the Misses Evans, was relieved when the real festivities began with the sports.

The Clare family did well, for Francis won the men's wheelbarrow race with the eldest Davis boy in the barrow whilst he did the pushing, and later still, Ada tore splendidly across the field in the girls' hundred yards, sash flying, nailed boots pounding, to win by a short head from the butcher's daughter. Dolly came second in the obstacle race, but was beaten by Emily Davis whose wiry skinniness negotiated ladder rungs and wriggled under tarpaulins with amazing dexterity.

Francis received half a crown, but Ada was delighted to have six yards of the unbleached calico which had recently covered the tea tables. It made stout pillow cases for the family which lasted for many years, and was considered by all to be a practical and most welcome prize.

At the end of the long golden day the little family made its way home. Young Frank slept in his wicker perambulator, and across the bottom was lodged the roll of calico. The lane was warm and scented with honeysuckle from the sun-baked hedges, and the smell of hay, lying ready to be turned when the labourers returned to the fields next day after the holiday, mingled with the other summer scents.

Tired Dolly, clinging to the pram for support, thought she would never forget such a wonderful day. 'Nothing ever happens in Beech Green,' she had heard people say. No one could say that now, was Dolly's last thought, as her dizzy head burrowed into the pillow beside Ada's. It was the most splendid thing that had ever happened in her young life.

Although Dolly, at nine years of age, was unconscious of the importance of the Jubilee and its times upon her outlook, yet looking back, as an old woman, she began to realise how deeply events and national movements had influenced even such a quiet life as her own. The Queen's celebrations had brought unaccustomed vivacity and loquacity to the country folk around her. Dolly, unusually excited by the stir, learnt more then about England's place in the world, her great men, her victories abroad and the reforms needed at home, than she had ever done before.

From Mr Finch she learnt of the vast areas of the world ruled over by their own Queen. From him she learnt of the Empire, following his pointer as it leapt from one red splash to another across the map of the world hung over the easel. She was told of the courage and military persistence of those who had subjugated the natives of those parts, and the benevolence of the great Queen whose laws now ruled them. She was not told of the feelings of those subjugated, but supposed that they were as happy to be in the Empire family as she was herself. Certainly the most splendid photographs of African chiefs, Indian princes, and the nobility of many far-flung territories taking part in the Diamond Jubilee celebrations, were cut from the newspapers and pinned up on the schoolroom wall where they were much admired by Queen Victoria's young subjects.

From the newspapers too, Dolly and Emily, both becoming avid readers, soon recognised the modern hero. He was a man of action, willing to tear up his roots and leave his country to explore unknown lands, to seek his fortune – in gold, maybe, in diamonds perhaps – to fight bravely, to dominate and to carry the British way of life to the unenlightened. He was a hero likely to be acceptable to boys as well as girls, for he was a colourful figure of wealth and power to those living amidst the pinching poverty of rural England at that time. The lot of the agricultural labourer grew worse weekly. The trek to find work in the towns continued. More and more white-collar workers struggled along in increasingly drab surroundings. It was small wonder that they craved colour and sensation to add excitement to their lives. The accounts of England's conquests overseas and the blaze of publicity which illuminated her leaders fired many a young man to join the army or to emigrate to those colonies whose exotic representatives marched in the Queen's processions.

The nineties needed sensation. The Diamond Jubilee was an occasion for national rejoicing, not only in the Queen, but in the nation's image as personified by her, proud, beloved, and a world-ruler. It was an image of Britain's greatness which was to remain with Dolly and her contemporaries. It gave them a deep sense of pride which would be needed to sustain them through many a change and the tragedy of two world wars. It gave them too a stability and a faith in ultimate victory which a later generation was to marvel at, deride, but secretly envy.

Later, Miss Clare was to see the follies and mistakes that had accompanied Britain's imperial policy during the nineties, but on that June night, after a shining day of rustic rejoicing, everything seemed wonderful to the little girl, with God in his heaven, the Queen on the throne, and the glory of an Empire everywhere around.

CHAPTER 9

THE friendship between Emily and Dolly deepened with time. They shared a passion for flowers, reading and little children, and were lucky enough to find plenty of each to keep them happy.

The woods on the hill to Springbourne, a neighbouring

village on the other side of the downs, were their hunting ground for flowers almost all the year round. They found wild snowdrops, violets, anemones, primroses and nodding catkins while the year was yet young. Later, bluebells and curling bracken fronds delighted them. Foxgloves and campion followed, and then, in the autumn, they had the joy of collecting hazel nuts and blackberries, as busily as the red squirrels that darted airily across the frail twigs high above their heads. Even in winter the wood offered treasures for those who cared to seek, and the two little girls would return carrying orange toadstools or lichen-covered branches in their cold hands.

Both children were fortunate too in having parents enlightened enough to give them a small patch of garden for their own cultivation. Most cottage gardens at this time were given over exclusively to the growing of vegetables for the family, and there was real need for this. Consequently, very few children had anywhere to play on their own territory, and fewer still were able to count a yard or two as their very own. Dolly and Ada shared a patch, and Emily had a much smaller one in her own garden. Here the children planted any seeds they could beg, and slips of plants given them by indulgent grown-up gardeners. The result was gay and unusual. Radishes and marigolds rioted together, a cabbage sheltered a clump of yellow pansies, and double daisies tossed their fringes beside mustard and cress.

They were lucky too with reading matter. Mr Finch, for all his pomposity and strictness, was a good teacher, and fostered any talent and interest that he saw. Books from the school library shelf could be borrowed, if brown paper covers were made for them and they were returned within a week. Often he lent a book from his own house, and this was greatly treasured. In this way Emily and Dolly were able to read more recent fiction than the Marryats, Mrs Ewings, and Kingsleys on the school shelf. Rider Haggard, Conan Doyle and Kipling were some of the new authors that the little girls met for the first time, and though there was much that escaped their understanding, the excitement of the stories swept them along in a fever of anticipation and made them long for the chance to see the strange foreign places there portrayed. Young though they were, they too had caught the fever for adventure which quickened their elders at this time, and they mourned the fact that they were female, and so never likely to have the opportunities of Allan Quatermain. Dolly's greatest moment came when Mr Finch presented her with a copy of *Three Men in a Boat*, which remained a favourite of hers for many years, though at its first reading she skipped all the moralising bits and the descriptions.

There were plenty of children, in their own families and their neighbours', to satisfy their interests, and mothers were glad to trust their toddlers to two girls who were so unusually sensible. Their sorties to the woods were usually in the company of Frank and another toddler or two straggling happily along behind them, or stuffed in an old pushchair and rattling over the uneven path.

'Fresh air's free,' the mothers used to tell them; 'you get as much of it as you can.' And out the children would be bundled, while cottage floors were swept and scrubbed, and the steel fenders and fire irons were polished with emery paper, and everything 'put to rights', as they said, in the few snatched minutes of freedom from their offspring. Consequently, there were always plenty of young children ready to join in games, or to be petted and admired by the older girls.

Looking back, Miss Clare saw how valuable all this unconscious training had been to her work as a teacher. The love of flowers and reading she passed on to many a country

child, and her own response to young children, protective and
warm-hearted, never failed her.

Friendship with Emily meant less dependence on Ada, and
now that the two sisters were growing older, the differences in
temperament became even more marked. Ada grew more
handsome as the years passed, and her boundless vivacity made
her attractive to the boys at Beech Green school as well as the
girls. Fearless and athletic, she could climb a tree or vault a
fence, despite her hampering skirts, as bravely as the boys, and
Ada Clare was known as 'a good sport'.

Francis Clare adored all his children, but his bonny Ada
became increasingly dear to him. Mary looked in some doubt
upon her firstborn. There were times when she was headstrong and disobedient, and Mary foresaw a difficult time
ahead when young men would enter Ada's life.

Sometimes Dolly was frightened by Ada's bold disobedience
of her mother; at other times she was grateful for some small
rebellion which proved successful and benefited them both.
The weekly dosing was a case in point.

As was the custom at that time in almost all households, the
Clare children were given a mild purgative, usually on Saturday
evening. Francis had been brought up to expect a teaspoonful
of a home-made concoction with nauseating regularity. His
mother chopped prunes, raisins, figs and dates, plentifully
sprinkled them with powdered senna pods and a little medi-
cinal paraffin oil and mixed it together to form a glutinous and
efficient purge. It had the advantage of being reasonably
palatable and wholesome, but Mary considered 'Grandma's
jollop', as the children called it, very old-fashioned, and
substituted castor-oil, which she disguised in hot lemonade.

It was Ada who called Dolly's attention to the suspicious
oily rings floating on the top.

'Don't you drink it,' she warned the younger child, in her mother's absence. Mary was at first persuasive, then unsuccessfully authoritative, and finally plain cross, as the two little girls flatly refused to drink the brew.

Francis only laughed when she told him.

'Give 'em Grandma's jollop then,' he suggested. 'They like that, so they say.'

But Mary tried another stratagem. On the following Saturday a plate of dates was offered to the children.

'This one hasn't got a stone in it,' said Dolly with surprise.

Her mother, busy ostensibly with darning, said briskly:

'Maybe it's got some grey powder inside instead.'

'That's right. It has,' agreed Dolly.

'You get some dates like that,' said Mary complacently. 'Some has stones and some has grey powder.'

They ate them unprotesting, thrilled to have such a treat as dates; but Ada discovered the trick before the next Saturday. Other children had grey powder administered in this form, she heard from her schoolfellows.

Fruit laxative tablets, called optimistically by Mary 'nice pink sweets', were tried next. Dolly and Ada held them in their mouths, pretended to swallow them, and then removed them when their mother was out of the room.

'Put 'em under the table ledge, quick!' whispered Ada, and there for several weeks a collection of sucked tablets grew, on a narrow ledge under the table top, well hidden by the red tablecloth.

At last came the day of open rebellion. Ada refused to take any form of medicine again.

'You'll be ill,' warned her mother. 'It's only taking these pills regular that's kept you and Dolly so fit and well. Your mother knows best now.'

'That she don't,' said Ada defiantly, tossing her bright hair.

'If you looks under the table ledge you'll see what we've done with 'em all this time. And we ain't come to no harm!'

The pink tablets were discovered, the two little girls sent to bed in disgrace, and Francis told all when he returned.

He hugged his vexed wife and restored her spirits.

'Well, she've told the truth. Their insides works all right without a lot of oiling, it seems. Let 'em off, my dear, and save a mint of money, and temper too.'

Thus Ada's battle, and Dolly's too, was won. These things happened when Frank was too young to be included in the ritual, but as soon as he was old enough he was told by his sisters just how fortunate he was to have escaped such horrors, and how thankful he should be to those who had smoothed the path before him.

If Mary had a favourite among her three children (and she stoutly maintained that she had not), then it was little Frank. He was darker in colouring than the two girls, who took after Francis. The dark bright hazel eyes that shone so lovingly upon his mother were the same colour as her own, and his hair grew as crisply. More open in his affection than her daughters, Frank charmed Mary by his frequent hugs and kisses, and many a smack was left unadministered because the knowing young rogue disarmed his mother with his blandishments.

'Make the most of him while he's yours,' observed Francis, watching the toddler on his mother's lap. 'He'll break plenty of hearts, I reckon, before he goes off to settle down and leave you.'

'You won't leave your mum, will you, my love?' said Mary, dancing him up and down.

Although she had learnt of the advent of the baby with mixed feelings, the joy which she felt in this boy lay largely in the feeling of future security which he brought, although Mary

herself was unconscious of this. The girls would marry,
Francis might die first: a son was an insurance against want and
loneliness, a joy to her now and a comfort for her old age.

When, in the autumn of 1899, the Boer War broke out, she
looked upon her three-year-old and gave thanks that he was so
young. Several young men from Beech Green had joined the
army to escape from hard times and to seek adventure. Some
were now in South Africa and Mary knew the anxiety which
gnawed at the hearts of their mothers. She prayed that her
Frank would never have to endure the dangers of war, nor she
the heartbreak of those who wait for news.

Christmas that year was a sad one, overshadowed by the
reverses of the army in South Africa. At the manor, the Evans
family were dressed in heavy mourning for the eldest son, who
had been shot from his horse whilst attempting to relieve
Ladysmith with General Buller's forces. The village was
stunned. This seemed to bring the war very near, and people
concerned themselves with the direction of the hostilities with
real anxiety. Should General Buller have suggested to White
that he surrendered Ladysmith? It seemed a terrible thing for
an Englishman to think of giving in. But then look at the loss
of lives? Look at poor Algy Evans and the Willett boy from
Fairacre and the Brown twins from Caxley! So the tongues
wagged, and wagged still faster when they heard that Buller
had been replaced by Lord Roberts who had lost his only son
in the same battle that took their own Algy Evans.

Queen Victoria was reported as saying at this time: 'Please
understand that there is no one depressed in *this* house. We are
not interested in the possibilities of defeat: they do not exist.'
These brave words were heartening, but did not completely
quell the fears that shook her less heroic subjects' hearts.

When Dolly visited the Davis' cottage one day, just after
Christmas in 1899, she found it clamorous with dismay.

Albert, the eldest son, had just announced that his New Year resolution was to join the army. Some of the family took his part, but his mother hotly attacked him. Dolly watched amazed the change in this smiling little Jenny-wren of a woman to a blazing fury.

'It's always what *you* wants,' she flared at the white, silent boy. 'Thinks yourself a hero, all dressed up in this new-fangled khaki to catch the girls' eyes! What about us? How's the family going to manage with your wages cut off?'

The boy began to explain haltingly, but was overborne. Dolly's heart bled for him as his mother's wrath gradually evaporated into self-pity.

'And what about a mother's feelings? Here I've brought you up from a baby, sat up nights when you was ailing, give you all you wanted, and what do I get in return? You fair break my heart, you do. You can't love me if you treats me like this.' She pulled a handkerchief from her sleeve and mopped the hot tears that coursed down her face. It was the old man of the house who opposed her most bravely. As he shook his black-gloved fist at her, his roars overcame the furious sobbing.

'You let 'un go. He's old enough to know what 'e wants, and you should be proud he's got the guts to want to fight. Don't I know his feelings? I went through the Crimean War – aye, and saw plenty of blood too, my own included, and would've died there but for Miss Nightingale, God bless 'er – and glad to, when we was fighting for the right thing. You women don't know half a man's mind. You try and keep 'im 'ere, tied down to your niminypiminy little ways and 'e'll 'ate you, and 'isself too, for the rest of his days.'

The boy cast a grateful look at the old man, and he continued more softly:

'There, gal, don't take on so. He'll be back before you knows where you are; and you can bet a fortune he won't go no

further than Salisbury Plain for many a long day. Let 'im 'ave 'is fling.'

Arguments flew for the rest of that week, but Albert was not to be deflected, and on the first day of 1900 he went to the recruiting officer in Caxley.

Emily and Dolly thought he was a hero, and defended his action enthusiastically. Here, in real life, was a happening as exciting as those they so often read about. Their interest in the war became redoubled, and they pestered old Mr Davis to tell them about his earlier war-time memories, but all his accounts, they discovered, soon turned to eulogising Miss Nightingale, whose personality had completely ensnared him.

'She's the most beautiful woman alive,' he told them, 'and the bravest. She never cared how rough or foul-mouthed we was to begin with – she soon altered all that. We fair worshipped her out there, and I see her once not long ago when I went to stay with a brother of mine at Claydon. There's a big house there that the Verneys own, and Miss Nightingale stays there sometimes with her sister. She was sitting with her in the garden and I stood behind a tree and looked at her, and looked at her. I thought to myself: "If ever a lady deserves a rest it's that one".'

His old eyes grew so ardent when he spoke of Miss Nightingale and her band of nurses that Dolly seriously considered the possibility of taking up nursing as a profession as she watched him. What could be more rewarding than to see love and gratitude flashing from the eyes of a soldier? A young one preferably, of course. Perhaps Albert Davis? Though, on second thoughts she did not want him hurt at all. And how becoming a nurse's uniform was! Dolly saw herself tripping lightly up and down a long ward, a veil floating behind her, the idol of her adoring patients. She was enchanted by the idea.

Enchantment ended a few hours later when little Frank was sick that evening and she was sent to clear up his cot. Sousing revolting bed linen in a tub of icy water, she realised, with devastating clarity, that nursing was not for her.

CHAPTER 10

DURING the first year of the new century, the object of prime importance at Beech Green school was a large-scale map showing the area in which the Boer War was being waged.

Each morning, before prayers, the boys would gather round

it, moving the little flags to show the day-to-day progress of the troops. Great was the rejoicing when besieged Ladysmith was finally relieved on February 28th, and greater still when, after 217 days of siege, Mafeking too was relieved in May.

Mr Finch was so infected with the national fever on this occasion that he let the children have a bonfire in the playground, and watched their wild dancing around it with an indulgent eye.

The most envied boy in the school was one who wore a tie of the new khaki colour decorated with dozens of tiny Union Jacks. The war, it seemed, was as good as won, as the summer wore on, and when, in the autumn of 1900, Lord Roberts and Buller came home to England, Beech Green felt sure that peace was not far distant.

'Your boy won't never get to South Africa,' they consoled Mrs Davis. 'Just a case of Kitchener clearing up the mess, and it'll all be over by harvest, you'll see.'

At the end of the summer term another excitement occurred. It was announced that Mr Finch was leaving and would take up a new appointment in a large school in the county town. This meant promotion, and his neighbours were quick to congratulate him.

The children were secretly glad to see him go. He wasn't a bad old stick, said some, but it would be good fun to have someone new who wasn't so strict. As one wag put it, in Dolly's hearing:

'Talk about the relief of Mafeking! I reckons it'll be the relief of Beech Green School when old Finch goes!'

The new headmaster came in the autumn. He was young and unmarried, but possessed a fiercely possessive mother who ruled the school house and her son as well.

Ada and the older girls were his slaves from the start. His fair wavy hair, worn a shade too long by country standards, and his pale face made him an object of interest and reverence. His clothes were much less formal than Mr Finch's had been, and he favoured big floppy ties in delicate pastel colours.

'Proper wishy-washy young feller', was what the men of Beech Green called the newcomer behind his back. But the women were inclined to take his part.

'He's just up-to-date, that's all. Very good thing too, to have someone who can teach the children without waving the cane at 'em all day,' they maintained.

His name was Evan Waterman, and he proved to be an ardent churchgoer, much given to genuflection and crossings during the services at Beech Green, which occasioned deep suspicions in the hearts of his Low Church neighbours. The vicar was delighted to have such a devout young man in charge of the school, and his visits there became more frequent and lengthy than ever.

'Lives in the parson's pocket,' grumbled old Davis one day, in Dolly's hearing. 'Don't trust that new chap no further'n I can see 'im! Too good to live, 'e be, mark my words!'

Mr Waterman had not been in school for a week before he told the children that he hoped he need never use the cane again, and to give emphasis to his words he threw it dramatically on to the top of a high cupboard where it lodged among a group of dusty wooden cubes, cones, spheres, and other geometrical shapes which had been undisturbed for years.

The rousing cheer which greeted this display might have warned a wiser man of perils to come, but Evan Waterman simply flushed with pleasure and told himself that he had won a place in his pupils' grateful hearts. Had he known it, it was not gratitude that enflamed those savage breasts, but the thought of a rollicking future where impudence and laziness would go unpunished. The boys winked merrily at each other, quivering with secret mirth. The girls gazed at their new headmaster with rapt devotion. In any case, they had seldom felt the cane, and had nothing to lose.

He told the children that he hoped they would look upon him as a friend, and would tell him of anything that perplexed or frightened them.

'I am here to help you,' he said earnestly, leaning forward in his desk with his pale blue tie flapping dangerously near the inkwell. The red faces of the older boys, choking with suppressed laughter at such antics, he attributed to natural bashfulness. He was determined to put into practice the new ideas in education, and to throw out the repressive methods which he saw had been those used by Mr Finch. To see the children curtseying and bowing to their elders shocked Mr Waterman seriously. The military precision with which the classes stood, turned and marched from the schoolroom to the playground appalled him. In the future, he told himself – and his astonished pupils – all would be freedom and light, and work would be done for the joy of doing it, not because he said so.

He might have known, poor fellow, that such drastic changes take time, and are bound to be accompanied with much trial and tribulation. Certainly the younger children benefited from this easier régime, and the fear that Mr Finch had aroused in them was never inspired by Evan Waterman's presence in their classroom.

The new infants' teacher, who had taken the place of Mrs Finch, was a robust young woman who cycled from Caxley daily on her new safety bicycle. She was a rosy-cheeked young Amazon, called Jenny North, and the village was quite sure that she would soon conquer Evan Waterman's heart and install herself as mistress of the school house in place of the dragon who lived there at present. This topic kept the village gossips engrossed for quite a fortnight, but – alas for their hopes! – the young woman was 'going steady' with a respectable draper in Caxley, and had eyes for no one else. She looked upon her headmaster's methods with a tolerant eye, but did not hesitate to administer a sharp slap upon her young sinners' legs, when her classroom door was safely closed. She and her charges understood each other well enough, and Beech Green parents soon realised that their young ones were getting on steadily under their new teacher.

About the older children they were less happy as the weeks went by. Gales of laughter and a few shouts could be heard from the schoolroom, where only Mr Finch's stentorian tones had been heard before. Rude rhymes were written on stable walls beginning:

Old Milk-and-Waterman
Lost the cane . . .

and the little girls came home, bright-eyed, with tales of kind Mr Waterman patting their hands and telling them they were growing up to be very pretty.

Francis Clare was present one day when Ada burst in from school and threw her books so carelessly on the table that they slid across the surface and crashed to the floor.

'Look out, my girl,' remonstrated Francis. 'That's your school books, you know.'

'Don't matter,' responded Ada carelessly, tossing back her bright hair. 'Mr Waterman says we can do some arithmetic or learn poetry, whichever we like. And he told me not to sit up too late over it, or I'd spoil my pretty eyes.'

She smirked as she repeated the words, and Francis looked at her steadily. Now, at fourteen, in her last term at school, she certainly was pretty, but it wasn't Mr Waterman's place to tell her so, thought Francis with rising anger.

'You don't want to listen to such foolishness,' said Francis.

'And your headmaster should know better than to encourage vanity. Pick your books up, and then go and help your mother.'

When the girls were safely in bed Francis spoke openly to Mary.

'I don't like that chap and I never shall. He's no business to lead them girls on so, and I shall have a word with the vicar about the way he's going on. The best thing we can do, my dear, is to get our Ada settled in a good job and let her leave as soon as it's fixed. No need to wait till Christmas. She's fourteen now and big enough to find a place.'

Mary Clare agreed.

'Mrs Evans was asking for her,' she said. 'It'd be nice to have her handy, and she'd be happy at the manor, I'm sure. I'll have a word with the child.'

'You do that, Mary,' said Francis, 'and I'll give that young feller a straight word or two. There's plenty of talk about him in the village – the work at school is going downhill fast, they say, and the boys just play the goat and get away with it. If you ask me,' continued Francis sturdily, 'a bit of straightforward soldiering wouldn't hurt that young Waterman.'

The next day Mary broached the subject of going into service with Mrs Evans at the manor. To her surprise, Ada was vehemently against it.

'I'm not being maid to no one,' said the girl violently. 'Why should I be at everyone's beck and call! I knows what it'd be! All the greasy cooking pots would be left for me to wash. All the back corridors and stone floors would be mine to scrub. I'd do the vegetables, and clean the mud out of the sinks, and squash the black beetles, and do the flues! Well, I'm not going to, then. I'm going to work in a shop – that's what I want to do!

'But you'd still be at everyone's beck and call,' pointed out Mary. 'And there's only one shop in Beech Green, and that don't want anyone to help.'

'It's Caxley I'm thinking of,' said Ada. 'I don't want to be buried alive in Beech Green all my life. I want to see things going on. There's plenty of shops in Caxley that'd take me on.'

'Well, we'll think about it,' said Mary, taken aback at the assurance of her firstborn. 'I'll talk to your dad tonight and we'll see if we can hear of something.'

Meanwhile, Francis had called at the vicarage and had a few words with the vicar about his new headmaster. To tell the truth, the good vicar himself was beginning to have some misgivings about the new appointment, and agreed to speak to Waterman that week.

'I'm taking my two girls away as soon as I can arrange it,' said Francis as he said his farewells on the vicarage doorstep. 'And you'll find that other folk in Beech Green will be doing the same, sir, unless things alter.'

And the vicar, watching the thatcher's broad back vanish between the Wellingtonias that lined the vicarage drive, sighed heavily. He recognised righteous wrath when he saw it.

To Dolly, now twelve years old, that autumn seemed a time of upheaval and change. She was amazed to hear from her father that he was making plans to transfer her to Fairacre School next term. For her part, she quite liked Mr Waterman, though not with the ardour that the older girls felt for him. Already gaining the cool wisdom that was to be her mainstay in life, the younger child recognised the headmaster's folly as well as his good intentions, but felt sorry that his overtures were so rudely flouted by the boys. She enjoyed his lessons, appreciated his love of poetry and nature, and was beginning to wonder if she too might be a teacher one day.

She knew little of Fairacre except that the school was much the same size as Beech Green's and that it stood near the church. The headmaster had been there for a year or two, had a grown-up family, a jolly, bustling wife who took the needlework lessons, and shared her husband's passion for the local hunt. They always walked a pair of hounds, which frequently burst joyfully into the schoolroom, and on the days when the hunt met near Fairacre, the schoolchildren were allowed to follow on foot. It all sounded happy enough, but it was strange, and Dolly did not like changes.

From her father's manner, though, she realised that the affair was settled, and she made no demur. Ada was found a modest post in the draper's shop in Caxley owned by Jenny North's young man and his father. This stroke of good fortune was brought about by Jenny herself, who recognised a quick bright assistant when she saw one, and knew that Ada's pretty face would attract more business.

It was arranged that the girl should live with Francis's parents and walk daily to the shop in the High Street, not far from the school which she and Dolly had first attended. Sunday was the only day of the week when she could get home, and the grandparents promised to bring her in their old trap or send her with an obliging neighbour.

'But what I really want,' said Ada, eyes shining, 'is a new safety bicycle like Miss North's. Then I could go from here each day, couldn't I, mum?'

'Ah well,' said Mary indulgently, 'you save your wages and see how it goes. I reckon you're a lucky girl to have everything fall out so nice for you.'

The house seemed very quiet without Ada's boisterous presence, and little Frank was promoted to her empty bed in Dolly's room. Dolly was glad of his company, although he was usually fast asleep when she crept up at night, a pink and white cherub with tousled dark curls.

He woke early, and Dolly first discovered her ability to weave stories to amuse the little boy. He liked best one about

a naughty child called Tom whose adventures continued in
serial form for weeks on end. Years later, Dolly Clare revived
Tom's adventures for the amusement of many schoolchildren.

Frank, at nearly four years of age, was increasingly dear to
Dolly. She took him with her wherever she could, and was
already looking forward to taking him to school at Beech
Green after Christmas, when the ultimatum had been given
about the move to Fairacre. Now someone else would have to
be found to take Frank to school, for Fairacre was too far away
for his short legs, and in any case, the teaching which he would
get with Jenny North perfectly satisfied Francis and Mary.
Time enough to think of Fairacre for young Frank, they told
each other, when he was big enough to go into the headmaster's class.

'And if I knows anything about it,' said Francis, 'there'll
be a different headmaster sitting in that chair by that time!'

Both parents thought a great deal about their son's future,
and Francis was delighted to find that, young as the child was,
he already showed an interest in the straw, the knives and hazel
spars which one day, Francis hoped, would be the tools of his
honourable trade.

They were all glad of the child's gay prattle during that
period of autumn gloom, for, besides Ada's absence, other
circumstances cast a shadow. The war, which had seemed all
but won in September, now took a turn for the worse, and
fighting flared up again, on a scattered front, and with renewed
bitterness.

As Christmas approached, anxiety grew. On December
22nd it was announced that thirty thousand more mounted
men would be sent overseas. Among them, this time, was
young Albert Davis, and there was much sadness in the little
home. It looked as if the Christmas of 1900 was to be as
gloomy as the year before.

The sight of her friend Emily, her face mottled with crying and her eyes puffy and red, brought home suddenly to young Dolly the widespread wretchedness of war, in contrast to the excitement and glory which had so enthralled her a year earlier. She pondered on this new revelation of war's grim side one morning in the Christmas holidays, as she stood by the kitchen copper, watching the clothes boiling gently, the suds sighing up and down like someone breathing. Death was a fearful thing and an ugly one. She remembered the horror of the corpses in the butcher's shop at Caxley, and shuddered. Only that morning she had come across a squashed wren on the road outside their gate – a small round pile of flattened feathers with its tail neatly erect upon it. She had watched that wren, for many weeks, running up and down and in and out of the thorn hedge, and rejoiced in its perky two inches of feathered vitality. And now it lay, stilled for ever, a pathetic scrap, as neat and tidy in death as in life.

To think that men could set out to reduce each other to that dreadful condition made the child feel cold with revulsion, as she prodded the steaming linen with the copper stick. It was bad enough to have Christmas overshadowed, to have to endure the loss of Ada's company, to face the ordeal of changing schools, and to see the Davises – and particularly dear Emily – suffer so, without this final overpowering horror of death to torment her.

Later, she wondered if those black thoughts had been something in the nature of a premonition. For, before a month had passed, death was to come very close to Dolly Clare, setting a grim mark upon that little household which even time itself could never completely remove.

CHAPTER 11

ONE morning in January 1901 Dolly awoke first. It was still dark and she could hear her father and mother moving about downstairs getting ready for the day. Usually, young Frank woke when they stirred and insinuated himself into Dolly's bed hoping for more stories.

But this morning he lay heavily asleep, drawing deep snoring breaths that at first amused his sleepy sister.

'Wake up, Frank,' she called at length. 'You're snoring like an old piggy!'

There was no reply.

Dolly began to whistle a tune that he called their 'waking up' song, a modified version of the army reveille, but there was no response from the sleeping child.

She climbed out of bed and padded across the cold ancient boards to peer at her brother. He seemed much as usual, as far as she could tell in the dim light, but when she put her hand on his forehead to push back his hair she found it hot and wet with sweat. Frightened, she ran downstairs to the lamp-lit room where the smells of breakfast rose from the stove.

'Frank's bad,' she told her parents, and followed them up the narrow staircase, shaking with cold and fear.

The candles were lit, and Mary and Francis leant over the bed. The child woke and smiled at them, and Dolly's heart was comforted.

'He don't look too bad to me,' said Francis. 'Keep him in bed today, my love. He's just got a bit of a chesty cold.'

'He will keep taking his scarf off,' said Mary anxiously. 'And it was that bitter yesterday when he was out in the garden.'

She looked at her son closely.

'D'you reckon we should get the doctor?' she asked hesitantly. Doctors cost money, and were not called unnecessarily to the Clare household. Besides, she did not want Francis to think her unduly pernickety, but Frank had never ailed anything before, and this seemed a severe type of fever.

'You let him lie there today,' repeated Francis. 'I'll get home in good time, and if he don't seem to have picked up, we'll send for doctor then.'

He kissed his womenfolk, bade them cheer up, and set off for work.

Frank slept most of the day, making the same alarming noise which had woken Dolly. Mary Clare's fears were calmed by Mrs Davis, who assured her that her own children had often suffered such symptoms, and a day in bed usually cured them.

'Believe me, my dear,' she told the anxious mother, 'that little 'un's all right. You knows what children are – up one minute, down the next. It's because he's the only boy you're worrying so. You see, tomorrow he'll be fairly.'

But when Francis came home that night he thought otherwise. Dolly had spent most of the day by the bedside, shaken by doubts, and only half-believing the comfort given by Mrs Davis. When she saw her father's face, her terror grew even greater.

'You cut along and get the doctor, Doll,' he said. And Dolly fled through the darkening village for help.

Bronchitis was diagnosed, and the child was moved downstairs to a makeshift bed on the sofa, drawn close to the stove where a kettle steamed for two agonising nights and days.

Mary never left his side for the whole of that time. She sat white-faced and very silent, ministering to the unconscious child's needs, and watching his every movement with awful concentration. When she spoke to Dolly, it was with such tenderness that the child could scarcely bear it.

Dolly was thankful that it was the school holidays and that

she could be there to help in the house and prepare the simple meals that, in fact, none of them had the heart to eat. Throughout the time that she worked, she prayed so vehemently that her head ached with effort. She tried to will God to make Frank better. Surely, she told herself, He wouldn't let him die! Not a little boy like that, who'd done nothing wrong! If men at war were killed, it was understandable, for they knew what they were doing, and God, she supposed, took some of them simply because men did die in wars. But there was no reason why Frank should be so sacrificed. Her distracted thoughts followed each other round and round in a demented circle, and all the time the prayers went up, and she saw them, in imagination, as an invisible vapour rising through the kitchen ceiling, and then the thatch, and finally the lowering grey winter clouds, spiralling their way heavenwards to that omnipotent Being in whose hands the life of little Frank was held.

On the third night, while Dolly slept above, the child slipped away, one hand in each of his parents'. He had never regained consciousness, but there was nothing to show that death was so close. He gave a little hiccup, and the harsh breathing which had dominated the house, quietly stopped. The silence had an icy quality about it, and for a stunned moment the stricken parents were powerless to move.

Then, across the motionless body of their son, their eyes met. Francis took Mary in his arms, and their bitter grief began.

The day of the funeral was iron-cold. A light sprinkling of snow whitened the churchyard, throwing the gaping black hole, awaiting the small coffin, into sharp relief.

In Dolly Clare's memory that day was etched for ever in stark black and white. The sad little family stood watching the coffin being lowered into the icy earth. A bunch of snowdrops trembled upon the lid, as frail and pure as the child within.

Clad in heavy mourning, Dolly remembered that other family she had pitied, so long ago it seemed, on the sunlit afternoon of the Diamond Jubilee. The bare black elm trees were outlined against a sky heavy with snow to come. Black spiked railings round a tomb nearby were tipped with snow, and from the church porch a row of footprints blackened the snow where the mourners' feet had passed. No colour, no warmth, no sunshine, no movement, comforted the spirit at that poignant parting, and Dolly remembered, with sharp intensity, the feeling of loss which had shaken her when she had kissed her brother's forehead, as cold and hard as marble, a few hours before. In the utter negation of death lay its chief terror.

In the weeks that followed, Mary Clare remained calm and unusually gentle with her family. After the first few hours of grief, she showed little sign of her loss. The neighbours shook their heads over her.

'She ought to cry, that she ought!' they told each other. 'That poor lamb's been buried over a week and she ain't shed a tear. 'Tis unnatural! She'll suffer for it, you'll see!'

There was certainly something uncanny, as well as heroic, about Mary's composure, but Francis was glad of it. His own tears were too near the surface for him to have endured his wife's emotion bravely.

It was perhaps as well for Dolly that her departure to Fairacre followed hard on the heels of this tragedy. Great was her joy when Emily told her that she too was starting at Fairacre School, and they could begin the new adventure together.

They set off through shallow snow on the first day of the term, Dolly clad in her mourning black and Emily, in gay contrast, in a bright scarlet coat which had once been her sister's.

They carried bacon sandwiches for their midday meal, and an apple apiece from Mrs Davis's store. The clatter of their strong nailed boots was muffled by the snow as they tramped along, and their breath steamed as they discussed what lay ahead.

'I knows about half of them anyway,' said Emily, seeking comfort. 'There's the Willets and the Pratts. I've played with them sometimes, and they said Mr Wardle's all right if you don't give him no cheek.'

'But what about Mrs Wardle?' asked Dolly.

'Rips up the sewing a bit,' said Emily laconically, jumping sideways into a fresh patch of snow which invited a few foot-prints.

'But I reckon they'll both be better than old Milk-and-Waterman.'

And Emily was right. On that first morning, as they sat together among their new school fellows, Dolly took stock of Fairacre School and began to feel the warmth of her surround-ings thaw the bleakness which had numbed her for the past few weeks.

A massive fire roared behind the fireguard, and though it could not hope to warm completely a room so lofty and so full of cross draughts, yet it was a cheering sight on a cold January day. Mr Wardle, warming his trouser legs before it, proved to be a hearty boisterous man who welcomed the newcomers, and bade his schoolchildren do the same.

He was that rare thing, Dolly discovered later, a happy man. Blessed with boundless energy, superb physique, a lively wife and four children now out in the world, Mr Wardle enjoyed his little domain and liked to see those in it equally happy. His recipe was simple, and he told it to the children over and over again:

'Work hard. Do your best, and a bit more, and you'll get on.'

Sometimes he put his recipe into a different form and read them a homily about the sin of Sloth, which he considered the most vicious one among the seven.

'If you start getting lazy,' he would
say, bouncing energetically up and down,
'you'll get liverish. And if you get liverish,
you'll get sorry for yourself. And that's
when the rot starts. Use your brain and
your body to the utmost, and the Devil
will know that he's beaten.'

He certainly set them all a fine example.
His teaching was thorough, exact and
lively. His spare time was taken up with
gardening, walking his hounds for miles
around the countryside, training the
church choir, and adding to a magnificent
collection of moths and butterflies. His authority was un-
questioned, unlike that of poor Mr Waterman at Beech Green,
and Dolly soon found herself responding to the vitality of this
man who could kindle a spark in even the stolidest of his
country scholars.

The children, perhaps because of Mr Wardle's example, seemed
friendlier than those at Beech Green, and Emily and Dolly, who
had secretly feared a little teasing and bullying, found no
antagonism. Nor were any remarks passed about Dolly's black
clothes, much to her relief. Although she did not know it until
many years later, Mr Wardle had already warned his children
about Dolly's loss and given them to understand that extra
kindness would be expected of them, and good manners most
certainly enforced, if his vigilant eye saw any shortcomings.

He was a man whose good heart and good head worked well
together. Quick to recognise a child's vulnerability, he never
descended to sarcasm and ridicule to gain his ends. Severe he
could be, and when he was driven to caning them the cane fell
heavily, but it rarely needed to be used. Work, exercise, fresh
air and laughter kept his charges engrossed and healthy; and

from Mr Wardle Dolly Clare learnt much of the ways of a good teacher.

About a week after their arrival, on January 22nd, 1901, Dolly and Emily sat with the rest of the big girls at one end of the main room, with needlework in their hands and Mrs Wardle's eye upon them.

It was called 'Fancywork' on the timetable, and each child had a square of fine canvas and skeins of red, blue, yellow and green wool on the desk in front of her. They were busy making samplers, using the various stitches which Mrs Wardle taught them. 'Fancywork' was a pleasant change from 'Plain Sewing' which involved hemming unbleached calico pillow slips with the strong possibility of seeing Mrs Wardle rip them undone at the end of the lesson.

The room was quiet. The boys at the other end were drawing a spray of laurel pinned against a white paper on the black-board, and only the whisper of their pencils as they shaded the leaves and carefully left 'high-lights', broke the sleepy silence.

It was then that the muffled bell of St Patrick's next door began to ring, and Mr Wardle, looking perplexed, hurried out to investigate. When he returned a minute later, his rosy face was grave.

'I have very sad news,' he told his surprised listeners. 'Queen Victoria is dead.'

There was a shocked silence, broken only by the distant bell and the gasp from Mrs Wardle, as her hand flew to her heart.

'All stand!' commanded Mr Wardle. 'And we will say a short prayer for the Queen we have lost, and the King we have now to rule us.'

Afterwards, it seemed to the children, the grown-ups made too much of this event, but they were wrong. Their lives were short, and to them the Queen had always been a very old lady near to death. To their parents and grandparents, who had known and revered her for all their lives, this passing of a great Queen was the end of the world they had always known. National mourning was sincere, and tinged with the bewilderment of children who have lost the head of a family, long loved and irreplaceable.

Dolly never forgot Emily's words to her as they crept quietly from the playground that day to make their way homeward.

'Won't Frank be pleased,' said Emily, 'to have the Queen with him!'

It was exactly what Dolly herself had thought when Mr Wardle had broken the news, and the comfort of hearing it put into words was wonderfully heartening. Certainly the shock of this second death was considerably lessened by Emily's innocent philosophy, and the thought of Frank's gain mitigated their own sense of loss.

It was not the first time that Emily had been of comfort to Dolly by her ability to come to terms with the unknown. In the years to come, her child-like simplicity and faith brought refreshment to them both.

Sixty or so years later, Miss Clare, half asleep in the shade of her plum tree, recalled that historic day, and its dark solemnity lit by Emily's touching confidence.

There certainly could be no greater contrast in the weather, thought Miss Clare, watching the heat waves shimmer across the sun-baked downs. In the border, the flaunting oriental poppies opened their petals so wide in the strong sunlight that they fell backwards to display the mop of black stamens at the centre. At the foot of the plant, Miss Clare's tortoise had pushed himself among the foliage, to escape from the June heat which even he could not endure.

She could hear the faraway voices of children at play, and guessed it must be about half past two, when Beech Green school had its afternoon break. Soon Emily would be with her again, as comforting and as hopeful as she had been on that bitter bleak day so long ago.

Miss Clare stretched her old stiff limbs in great contentment, revelling in the hot sunshine and the joy of Emily's coming. Looking back, she saw now that an age had closed on the day that Mr Wardle had called them to prayer, and she who since then had seen many reigns, could imagine the impact which Victoria's passing had made upon her parents' generation.

But for Dolly the twelve-year-old child, that day had been chiefly a turning-point in her own happiness. She could see now, sixty years later, that several things had contributed to the sudden lightening of her misery. Mr Wardle's infectious vitality, new surroundings, work praised and encouraged, had all helped together to raise the child's spirits from the depths into which her brother's death had cast them. The natural buoyancy of youth and time's healing powers added their measure of restoration, but it was Emily's homely words which had really set her free at last. It was as though the Queen had taken Dolly's burden upon herself by entering into that unknown world where Frank already waited, and, fanciful though the idea seemed a lifetime later, yet it still seemed touching in the strength and hope it had given to a sad little girl who had needed comfort sorely.

'Ah! It's good to grow old,' said Miss Clare, contemplating that pitiful young figure across the years, 'and to know that nothing can ever hurt you very much again. There's a lot to be said for being seventy!'

And turning her face gratefully to the sun, she continued to wait, lapped in warmth and contentment, for the coming of Emily.

PART THREE *Fairacre*

CHAPTER 12

FROM the first, Dolly Clare liked Fairacre. It was a compact and pretty village, grouped charmingly about its church, unlike Beech Green, which straggled along the road to Caxley. Some of the cottage roofs had been thatched by her own father, since they had come to live nearby, and still shone golden in the sunshine. More ancient roofs had weathered to a silvery grey, while others, more venerable still, sagged thinly across their supports and sprouted with green patches of moss and grass.

Not all the cottages were thatched. More than half were tiled with small tiles of a warm rosy brown which combined with the weathered brick to give a colourful appearance to the village. A few large houses, built in the reigns of Queen Anne and the early Georges, glowed with the same warm colour among their trees, and little Dolly Clare grew to love the vicarage, which could be seen plainly from the playground of Fairacre school, admiring its graceful fanlight over the front door, and the two great cedar trees which stood guard before it.

Fairacre, in those Edwardian days, was rich in fine trees, planted to give shelter, no doubt, from the roaring winds which swept the whaleback of the downs above it. Limes and horse-chestnuts shaded gardens, and clumps of magnificent elms sheltered the cattle and horses in the farm meadows. Close by the school, protecting both it and the school house, towered more elm trees, in which a thriving rookery clattered and cawed, and several of the neighbouring farms had leafy avenues leading to their houses. There was much more ivy about at that time. The dark glossy leaves muffled many a garden wall and outhouse, and added a richness to the general scene. When, in later life, Miss Clare looked at old photographs of the Fairacre she had known as a child, she realised how denuded of trees the village had become within her lifetime.

She and Emily loved it from the start. Their spirits rose as they turned the bend and approached the church and school. It was almost three miles to walk each morning, but the two little girls were quick to find lifts with obliging carters and trades-men, and rarely had to walk both ways in the day. Dolly, who had been so frightened by the size of Bella on the day of the move from Caxley, now treated these great-hearted horses with affection and complete trust as she scrambled up from shaft or wheel hub to her high perch beside some good-natured driver who had taken pity on the two young travellers.

In all weathers, riding or walking, they traversed the familiar road. They looked out for the first wild flowers of spring, the pink wild roses that starred the summer hedges, and the bright beads of autumn berries. They watched the birds building nests, and could tell to a day when the eggs would hatch. They knew where a badger lived, and where a white owl would appear as they plodded home on a murky winter after-noon. Those three miles grew as familiar and as well-loved as the faces of their mothers. There was always something new, something beautiful, something strange, to find daily, and the two children learnt as much from their close scrutiny of banks and hedges as they did in the busy classroom at Fairacre school.

As Dolly and Emily neared the end of their schooldays, in the early part of Edward VII's reign, they found that one or the other was frequently called upon to walk from Mr Wardle's room to the infants' room next door in order 'to give a hand', as Mr Wardle always put it, to the teacher in charge.

They were now called monitors, and with one or two other children of fourteen, undertook a number of daily jobs in the running of the school. Numbers thinned after the age of twelve, for those who could pass an examination in general proficiency were allowed to leave, and farmers were eager to employ these young boys now that labour was difficult to obtain. This meant that those over twelve who were left behind were often lucky enough to get closer attention from their headmaster. Mr Wardle looked upon Dolly and Emily as promising pupil teachers of the future, and gave them every opportunity of learning the rudiments of the job under his roof.

Both girls enjoyed their time with the babies. Miss Taylor, a wisp of a woman with two protruding front teeth which were the only outstanding feature of an undistinguished appearance, was glad to delegate some of her duties.

'You take the little boys, dear,' she would say to Dolly, 'and you can manage the girls, Emily, while I hear the big ones read.'

And so, to a background of young voices chanting round the teacher's desk, Emily and Dolly would squat on low chairs by their charges and show them how to write capital letters on their slates, holding small hot hands within their own while wet slate pencils traced uncertainly the mysteries being explained.

Sometimes, when Miss Taylor wanted peace in which to mark sums or tidy cupboards, Dolly would perch on the high chair before the class and tell them one of the stories about naughty Tom which had once delighted little Frank. It warmed her heart to see the joy with which the children listened, and the company and affection of these babies did much to soften the blow of Frank's death.

It was no surprise to the girls when one afternoon Mr Wardle asked them to stay behind to talk about training as pupil teachers. It was a golden June afternoon with the weather-cock on St Patrick's ablaze in the sunshine against a clear blue sky. Their schoolfellows' cries died rapidly in the distance, for hay-making was in progress and the children were racing to join their fathers and big brothers in the meadows.

Emily and Dolly stood demurely in front of Mr Wardle's great desk, eyeing the massive brass ink stand and the array of pens.

'Well, would you like it?' asked Mr Wardle after he had outlined the training involved.

'I think I should,' said Emily hesitantly. Her grey eyes were clouded with concentration. A wisp of dark hair cleaved to her damp forehead. Volatile and exuberant by nature, Emily was pondering earnestly on her ability to stick to a course for four years and then to the profession to which it led. She liked children, she liked the idea of teaching them, but would she tire of it? She raised perplexed eyes to Mr Wardle's lively blue ones.

'You'll like it more every year,' promised Mr Wardle, seeing the child's doubts. 'You'll make a very good teacher in time.'

He turned to Dolly questioningly.

'I will,' said the child steadily. She might have been taking her vows, thought the schoolmaster, both touched and amused by the calm assurance with which she declared herself. It was strange that on this occasion the more timid of the two should be so confident. With a flash of insight, he recognised in that moment, that he was in the presence of someone who would become a much greater person than he would ever be, and he felt unaccountably humble.

'You're a born teacher,' he said quietly, and turned the key in his desk drawer to bring the interview to a close.

Together the three emerged into the dazzling sunlight.

'Tell your fathers that I have spoken to you about this,' said Mr Wardle, 'and ask them to come and see me. Meanwhile, think it over well. You don't want to spend your whole life regretting a decision. Take plenty of time to make up your minds.'

He watched their figures dwindle into the distance. The heat waves shimmered across the lane, blurring the outlines of their pale print frocks and wide straw hats. One of them, he thought, half-closing his eyes against the brightness, has given her mind to it already – and her heart and soul too. He only hoped that she would find as much happiness as he had himself.

Strangely moved and elated, he crossed the shade of his garden and entered the school house.

In the following September the two girls returned to Fairacre with the status of pupil-teacher. This meant that they helped Mr Wardle and Miss Taylor, and under their guidance prepared and gave lessons occasionally, generally making themselves useful. Twice a week they went into Caxley for evening classes, and occasionally they attended an extra class, or a demonstration lesson by a qualified teacher, on a Saturday morning.

Both girls were excited by their promotion. They enjoyed the trips to Caxley, and knew that they were luckier than most village children in continuing their education after the age of fourteen. To be sure, the work expected of them was fairly simple – Arithmetic, English, Geography, History and Nature Study – only a little more advanced than Mr Wardle's final lessons with his top class, but it was stimulating to see different pupils and to be taught by a variety of men and women.

Francis and Mary were pleased with Dolly's choice of career. Their shy one, it seemed, was blossoming. Mary helped

Dolly to lengthen her skirts and to dress her soft hair in a top knot in a manner suitable to her new dignity. Emily's dark braids were now worn wound about her head, and the two girls spent much of their time adjusting each other's hair pins. The conversation on the way to Fairacre these days dealt with fashions rather more than education.

They both longed for 'low shoes' instead of the stout laced boots which they were still obliged to wear. The Misses Evans, also in their teens, were lucky enough to wear shoes with straps every day of their lives, and on high days and holidays, so Dolly heard, they had real silk stockings to wear with them. They surveyed their own cotton-clad legs, terminating in the loathsome boots, with acute disfavour.

On the evenings that they went to evening classes they eyed the young women of Caxley, who appeared to their un-sophisticated eyes as positive fashion plates. Sometimes a carriage would rattle past, bearing a beautiful lady, on her way home from a tea party, wearing one of the delicious large Edwardian hats smothered in tea roses and with clouds of veiling tied beneath the chin. Dolly and Emily gazed with wonder. Would they ever be able to have a hat as adorable as that?

Getting to Caxley was a problem. Mr Wardle took them in on Tuesday evenings when he went to play chess with an old friend, and brought them home again. He owned a small governess cart, and it was a tight squeeze to get even such slim people as Dolly and Emily into it with sturdy Mr Wardle taking up more than half the room. On Thursday evenings they relied on the corn merchant's waggon which had been delivering goods in the Beech Green area all day, but this arrangement had its drawbacks, for the driver was a slow, ambling fellow, and the girls were in a ferment of anxiety until they were dropped at the Institute in Caxley High Street.

They returned home in style on Thursdays, for one of the women teachers, the daughter of a prosperous grocer in the town, had the use of her father's carriage and spanked along the lane to Beech Green when the lessons were over.

It was Ada who was responsible for solving this problem of transport in an indirect way. Growing prettier every year, with bright bold eyes and burnished hair, Ada had many admirers. The young men of Caxley were frequent customers at the general draper's where she worked, calling in to finger ties or to try on one of the dashing new straw boaters, while their eyes wandered over the pretty assistant. It was no wonder that old Mr and Mrs Clare grew anxious about this wayward grandchild. Despite their protestations, Ada came home later and later in the evening, and they felt powerless to control her. They spoke plainly to Francis about it one Sunday when they spent the day at Beech Green.

The girls had been sent out with a message while the problem was talked over. Francis was greatly perturbed.

'She'll have to live here,' he said firmly. 'Ada's our child, and we must see to her. 'Tisn't right that you should be bothered with her feckless ways at your time of life.'

'We'll see if Mrs Evans can have her there to work,' promised Mary. 'There's no way for her to get to Caxley every day, and maybe she's better in the village.'

The old man looked dubious.

'She won't take to it kindly, that I do know,' he said. 'And, to be fair, the girl's doing well at the shop, and they want to keep her.'

'Well, she can't get there,' said Francis, 'so that's that.'

'Your father and I,' said old Mrs Clare, 'have been thinking about that. You tell them, my dear,' she nodded to her husband.

'If you're agreeable,' said Mr Clare, 'I'd like to buy both girls one of these new safety bicycles apiece. They may as well have their little something now, when they need it, as wait for me to go to my grave and then get a pound or two. What'd you say, lad?'

'I'd say,' said Francis, with feeling, 'that they're two real lucky girls, and Mary and me'd be proper thankful to you.'

Mary was looking a little apprehensive.

"Tis real kind of you,' she said earnestly, 'but – but d'you think they'd be safe? I mean, Caxley's a busy place. They might get knocked down, or run into something if they couldn't manage the machines—'

Francis broke in upon his wife's misgivings.

'I'll see they learn to manage 'em before they goes to Caxley,' he assured her. 'You tell 'em the good news when they comes in, dad, and watch their eyes sparkle! You'll get plenty of kisses for this!'

'I don't want kisses or thanks,' said the old man, although he looked pleased at the thought, 'but they're good girls, and I'm glad to do it for them.'

And so it came about that once again Ada and Dolly shared a bedroom and set off each morning on their marvellous bicycles, one to Caxley and the other to Fairacre; and on Tuesdays and Thursdays Dolly rode proudly into Caxley to the evening classes, independent of lifts and free to come and go whenever she liked.

Only Emily was sad, and that sadness did not last long, for Mrs Evans remembered an ancient bicycle propped in an out-house and lent it to the girl for as long as she needed it. Pedalling along together, the wind playing havoc with their insecure coiffures and their long skirts, the two friends felt that life could hold no greater joy.

Francis Clare was delighted to have both his daughters at home again. His gay Ada had always been his secret favourite, and he was glad of her boisterous presence for Mary's sake.

Since the death of Frank, Mary had become much quieter. She rarely spoke of the child, and shrank from any mention of him by Francis. It was only to be expected, Francis told himself at first. The wound was still fresh and any attention to it gave pain. But as the years passed it seemed unnatural to Francis to remain so silent about the tragedy which had smitten them both so cruelly.

Every week Mary made her way to the grave and put fresh flowers upon the pathetically small green mound. She went alone, and this hurt Francis. She chose her time, when Francis was at work, and when he remonstrated gently with her, the tightening of her lips and stricken look in her eyes were enough to silence him. If only he could thaw her, he told himself, if only she would speak of her grief, then it could make things so much easier for both of them. As it was, he dared not hurt her more, and could only hope that the passing of time would bring them both comfort.

Ada's good spirits lightened the little cottage and Francis rejoiced in her vivacity. What if the boys did look at her in Caxley? Who could blame them? Ada had her head screwed on the right way, thought Francis, and knew how to behave herself. It was only right that she should attract young men at her age, and with her pretty ways. To tell the truth, he was half in love with her himself, seeing again the beauty that had been Mary's in years gone by.

So he comforted his wife when she wondered if they should be stricter with their lively first-born,

'There's safety in numbers, my love,' he said. 'Ada won't do anything silly. She may be a bit flighty. What girl at seventeen isn't? But she'll make some young man a good wife, you'll see.'

He spoke fondly, thinking of the years immediately ahead when Ada would still be a daughter in his house, with the possibility of marriage far ahead in the future. He did not see the flicker of doubt that passed across his wife's face.

CHAPTER 13

WHILE Ada enjoyed the bustle of life in Caxley High Street, and felt her spirits lift as she skimmed on her bicycle towards the town, Dolly found quiet satisfaction in the remote tiny world of Fairacre.

The school's setting was sheltered and peaceful. In those days rough turf surrounded the building, with a stone-flagged path leading to the road, and another to the school house. In summer this little green was white with daisies, and the bigger girls showed the younger ones how to make daisy chains with a pin, or a sharp thumb nail. Later, plantains sent up their tough stalks and knobbly heads, and the children used to pluck these and play 'knocking heads off' with skill and energy.

The writhing roots of the clump of elm trees provided more amusement for the babies, who contrived houses and shops in the spaces, and a steep bank which sloped into a field below the trees provided numerous slides in wet or dry weather.

On the grass, under the shade of the trees, stood a bucket of water. This was replenished daily by Mr Wardle, from his own well, and was the only drinking water for the school.

'Tastes a bit funny in the afternoon,' Dolly Clare heard one child say to another.

'Ah! But mornin's it's lovely!' replied the other fervently, obviously grateful for small mercies.

It was Dolly's duty to watch the children during the dinner hour. In the summer, they sprawled on the grass with their hunks of bread with a bit of cheese or bacon to help it down. Sometimes a few radishes or lettuce leaves were added to the meal, when they were in season, and in the autumn plenty of fine apples, plums and nuts were carried to school in the children's dinner bags. Washed down with a swig from the tin mug standing by the 'old bucket', it all tasted good to country children.

In the winter the desks were dragged forward nearer the blazing fire, and the children ate their meal with one eye on a large kettle which lodged on a trivet. Dolly and Emily made cocoa for them all, ladling a spoonful into the cups brought from home and adding a wobbly stream of boiling water from the heavy kettle. There was no charge for this, for years before, in the bitter winter of 1881, the managers had decided to provide this beverage from their own purses, and the kindly custom continued. A jug of milk was sent over daily from the farm near the church, and brown sugar was kept in a great black and gold tin which had come from China years before, to find an alien home at Fairacre. For many of the children the cocoa was the most nourishing part of their meal, for times were still hard for the agricultural labourer, and bread formed the major part of the contents of the school satchels, Dolly noticed.

School began at nine, and ended at four, so that for most of the year Dolly and Emily cycled home in the light. Only at the end of the Christmas term and the early part of the Spring one, when the oil lamps were lit from a long taper and shed meagre pools of light upon the children's heads below, were Dolly and Emily obliged to fix lamps to their bicycles and pedal through the dark lane behind the two wavering beams.

Dolly found the work absorbing. By nature she was methodical, cool-headed and patient. The children responded to her quiet ways with trust and affection. But it was for Emily that they showed most enthusiasm. Her quick wits, her humour, and her ready laugh made the children too excitable for Mr Wardle and Miss Taylor's liking. When Emily took a class into the playground to play 'Cat and Mouse' or 'Poor Jenny Sits A-Weeping', the shrieks would penetrate the stout schoolroom walls, and Mr Wardle, intercepting sly grins among his pupils, would stalk forth to call for stricter discipline outside.

'Ticked off again!' Emily would sigh, as they cycled home. 'I wish I could keep them as quiet as you do, Dolly.'

'They can do with livening up,' answered Dolly. 'I think they're kept a bit too meek indoors, and then they get wild as soon as they get outside. But, there you are, that's how Mr Wardle wants it, so we must do as we're told.'

'But just wait till we're headmistresses!' laughed Emily. 'We can do as we like then with the children.'

The possibility seemed so remote to the two young girls that they treated it with amusement. They might teach for a few years, they supposed, and enjoy it very much, but marriage, they felt sure, would one day claim them – marriage to someone as yet unknown, for all the known young men were far too familiar and dull to consider – and then another way of life would begin for them.

And so, happy in the present, and with vague and happy dreams of the future, Emily and Dolly passed the years of their pupil teaching in the long golden afternoon of Edward's reign, with never a thought of the shadows of war which crept slowly but inexorably nearer to their small bright world.

One June evening, about this time, Dolly came out alone from the evening institute in Caxley High Street. Emily was at home with a feverish cold. As she mounted her bicycle she caught sight of Ada in the distance, strolling some way ahead, on the arm of a thickset young man.

Dolly had heard Ada say that morning that she would be late home all the week as they were getting stock sorted ready for the summer sales. Had she finished, Dolly wondered, or had the task been fictitious?

The couple progressed slowly. They were deeply engrossed, and Dolly pedalled equally slowly to keep behind them. There was a look on Ada's face which she had never seen there before. It was a dumb, adoring look, quite unlike the bold flirtatious glances with which Dolly was familiar. The young man's arm crept round Ada's waist and they turned down a side lane towards the river.

Dolly trundled home much perturbed. She had recognised the young man, as he turned, as the son of a local publican. Though the father was respected, it was general knowledge that he had hopelessly spoilt his only child who was allowed too much money and too much licence. Harry Roper, thought the youthful Dolly, must be quite old – twenty-five at least – and Ada knew, as well as she did, that there were dozens of pretty girls, in Caxley alone, who had been as besotted as Ada now was, and who later had regretted their infatuation.

Cycling along the warm lane, with her eyes half-shut against the clouds of gnats, Dolly pondered. It was unlike Ada to lie to her mother. Then again, it was unlike Ada to be so secretive about her escorts. This affair was obviously more serious than the others, and Dolly did not like it,

She decided to say nothing to her parents, nor to Ada. But she was uncomfortably guilty that evening in her parents' presence, and glad to escape early to bed. There she lay, anxious for Ada's safe return, but it was past eleven o'clock before the girl crept upstairs, and by that time Dolly was sound asleep.

This escapade had its sequel, for the next day Francis met a friend who had been in Caxley the night before.

'Saw your girl last night,' he said brightly, his face alight with the pleasure of tale-telling.

'Oh yes,' answered Francis, observing the note of happy anticipation. 'She'd been to evening class.'

'Not this one hadn't!' asserted the friend inelegantly. 'Behind the bar of "The Crown" she was, and served me with a pint, too.'

Francis was completely taken aback, but with a country-man's caution did his best not to show it.

'I must be getting along,' he said, collecting his thatching shears and making towards the ladder.

''Bye,' said the other, setting off in the other direction, well pleased with the encounter.

Francis watched him go, and leant back against the ladder to consider this unsavoury piece of news. He was shocked by more than one aspect of it. In the first place, it looked as though Ada had deliberately lied about staying late for the sale. It also seemed that she was mixed up in company of which he had no knowledge. But worse still was the thought that she had appeared openly in a public bar. This hurt Francis deeply. She had disgraced them all.

Francis liked his pint now and again, and enjoyed his local pub, but at a time when drunkenness was rife and the wretched results were everywhere around, the idea of women, and particularly his own young daughters, being seen in a public house, was horrifying. His parents had been strict teetotallers, and he had been brought up to consider public houses as dens of depravity. If word of Ada's escapade ever reached her grandparents, it would be the end of them!

And what was the publican thinking of, to let a young girl serve in his bar? Francis grew belligerent at the thought, and found himself snapping the shears viciously.

'Best get on with my work,' he said aloud to a prowling cat. 'But I'll have a word with that young lady tonight. Maybe I'm too soft with her.'

He mounted the ladder and attacked the straw with unusual savagery.

Ada did not trouble to deny anything. She was in a hard, bold mood, offhand and insolent, calculated to send her parents into a frenzy. Dolly, cleaning her shoes in the kitchen, trembled for her sister. Mary was torn between tears and an overpowering desire to box the girl's ears, but Francis handled the affair competently.

'What's wrong with bringing the young man here?' asked Francis. 'If you like him well enough, let's see him. He'll come if he thinks anything of you.'

'Everyone's against him,' protested Ada, 'and you're the same. You haven't even seen him but you tell me I oughtn't to go out with him. And I don't see why I can't go to his home. He can't help living in a pub.'

'He don't live in the public bar,' said Francis shortly, 'and that's where you were – and serving too. His father could get into serious trouble for that, and he knows it.'

Ada's face flamed scarlet.

'I hates this place! Full of a lot of tittle-tattlers with nothing better to do than make trouble! But they shan't stop me seeing him – and neither will you!'

Francis kept his temper with difficulty.

'See here, Ada. I'm your father and I must do the right thing by my own daughter. You're young yet—'

'I'm nearly nineteen,' Ada burst in, 'and he's twenty-five, and we're going to be married as soon as we can.'

There was silence for a moment in the little room, then Francis spoke gently.

'I'd like to have heard about that from him first. The sooner I see this young man the better, I reckons, and his dad, too.'

'You don't understand—' began Ada, with a wail.

'Your mother and me has both been in love, you know,' commented Francis dryly. 'We don't want it explained to us. All we're saying is: don't do nothing in a hurry. If you've got any sense at all you'll keep away from him for a bit until I've seen him.'

'Oh, you *old* people!' expostulated Ada, flinging out of the room. Dolly heard the thud of her feet on the stairs and the creak of the bed as she flung herself upon it.

Francis and Mary exchanged hopeless looks.

'Well,' said Francis heavily, 'I'll go and thin my carrots. Need a bit of fresh air after that. Let her simmer a bit, my dear, and then you see what you can do with her. Proper headstrong hussy she's getting!'

'She always was,' said Mary candidly, to her husband's departing back.

The next day Francis made his way to 'The Crown' to see the publican. He did not relish the interview, but it had to be faced, and a steady anger helped his determination. He found his anger evaporating, as the meeting lengthened.

Mr Roper knew nothing, he said, of Ada, although he had seen his son with a girl in the parlour. His wife was about at the time, and he himself was busy with a party of travellers. He had been obliged to go into the yard to arrange stabling for their horses and had knocked on the parlour window and told Harry to attend to the bar. He was as upset as Francis to hear the news, he said; and Francis believed him.

They talked straightforwardly of the affair, and agreed to speak to their children again. If marriage was what they wanted, then Harry would call upon Francis at once.

'But if he's lukewarm,' said Francis honestly, 'you can warn him off. I'm in no mind to lose our Ada anyway, and she'll have plenty of choice.'

They parted civilly, and Francis returned to Beech Green with a more contented mind.

But for Dolly, this family row had particular significance. On the fateful night when the storm had broken Dolly crept to bed, praying that Ada would be asleep or content to lie silent. She herself was in such a turmoil of doubts and fears that she craved nothing but the unconsciousness of sleep.

But Ada was awake and in an ugly mood. She lay in bed watching Dolly undress by the light of a candle.

'I suppose you're glad I've been found out?' she said, speaking low so that their parents would hear nothing through the thin wall which divided the two rooms.

'Ada!' cried Dolly, cut to the quick.

'Ada!' mimicked her sister in a spiteful squeak. 'You know you were watching us – sneaking along on your bike! I saw you!'

'I couldn't help it—' began poor Dolly.

'And I bet you told mum as soon as you got home, that I wasn't sorting stock. Wanting to make me out a liar.'

'And are you?' asked Dolly, with a flash of spirit.

'Yes, I am then,' said Ada defiantly. 'You're driven to it in this mean rotten place. And I don't care! When you're in love you'll do anything!'

Dolly was shocked into silence. With trembling hands she hung the last of her clothes on the back of the chair, blew out the candle, and slid into her cold bed. The dreadful words beat in her brain – words all the more sinister from their sibilant whispering. 'When you're in love you'll do anything!' Lie to your parents? Shout abuse at them? Attack your sister with false accusations? Was this what love did to you?

She remembered Mr Waterman reading poems about love to his callous young pupils. Surely he had told them that love was ennobling and fired people with all that was good and beautiful? Love had not done that to Ada, it seemed.

She summoned all the courage and calm she could, amidst the tumult and the darkness, and spoke pleadingly.

'Ada, you don't really mean that. You're just upset. Try to go to sleep.'

Ada gave a hard, harsh laugh. It sounded like the cackle of a jay in the dark room, and it sent shivers down Dolly's spine.

'Don't you soft-soap me! You're a sneak, and I know it. And I mean every word I say. What do you know about being in love, anyway? You only got me into trouble because you're jealous – and that's the honest truth, Dolly Clare!'

The vicious whispering ceased as Ada thumped over towards the wall. Exhausted with emotion she fell asleep almost immediately, but Dolly lay, appalled and icily awake, until the dawn came.

During that long terrible night she came to realise that the rift which had been widening so steadily between Ada and herself was now too wide for any successful bridge. Gone were the days when Ada was always right, when Ada led and she followed, and when Ada – the bright, the beautiful, the brave – could count on her adoration and obedience.

Nothing would ever be quite the same again. The words had been said, the cruel blows given. Dolly felt that even if she could come at last to forgive, she could certainly never forget.

She fell into sleep as the cocks began to crow, and woke, two hours later, leaden-eyed, to a world which had lost some of its brightness for ever.

CHAPTER 14

LOOKING back across the years, as she lay half-dozing in the sunny garden, old Miss Clare marvelled that she should remember that wretched night so clearly. Was it true, she wondered, that she had been jealous of Ada's popularity with the young men? She had not realised it at the time. She had been furious and severely shaken by Ada's spite. But was there an element of truth there which the youthful Dolly unconsciously recognised?

Certainly her interest in boys was remarkably small at that time, Miss Clare remembered, and smiled to think of her first 'walking out', which occurred a little before Ada's escapade.

It was, not surprisingly, with Emily's brother Albert. He was now a corporal and a very fine figure in uniform.

When he came home on leave the family made much of him. Mrs Davis, all passion spent, was now proud to show off Albert in his khaki, and basked in the congratulations of her neighbours when he accompanied her about the village or took her shopping in Caxley.

He was a quiet, happy boy, pleased to be back in the overcrowded cottage but secretly a little lonely when the rest of the family were out upon their various ploys during the day. He wandered round Beech Green, leaning on a gate here and there to chat with men gardening or women hanging clothes. He stopped to talk to old school-mates, as they cut back hedges or turned the plough at the end of a long furrow, and felt mingled pride and guilt at the envy which he saw in their eyes.

'It ain't all beer and skittles,' he assured his questioners, almost apologetically. 'Sometimes I reckons you chaps has the best of it.' But he knew he was not believed. To the stay-at-homes, he had the glamour which a uniform and travel give.

To have some purpose for his meanderings, Albert frequently strolled towards Fairacre to meet his sister and Dolly on their way home from school. He was fond of them both, and a little sorry for Dolly, whom he considered overshadowed by Ada. If he had been bolder he might have approached Ada himself, but he knew that she was besieged by young men, and was afraid that he might be rebuffed. He felt safe with Dolly, and asked her one day if she would like to go to Caxley with him on the next Saturday. Somewhat surprised, Dolly agreed.

It was all very innocent and pleasant. They cycled together to the town, Albert on Emily's bicycle. It was a blue and white March day of strong sun and wind. Dolly bought some crochet cotton and a new hook, a pound of sprats which her mother wanted, and two ounces of cabbage seed for her father. Albert accompanied her into the shops, watching gravely over her purchases, and buying some cold wet cockles in the fishmonger's as a present for the Davis family's supper.

The fish was put into a small flat rush bag which was secured with a skewer. As the afternoon wore on it grew dark with dampness and decidedly smelly, but the two were in great spirits and felt very daring as they took their burden into a tea shop in Caxley High Street and Albert ordered ices.

'What would you like to do?' asked Albert, as they tinkled their spoons in the glass dishes.

'I don't really know,' said Dolly truthfully. 'I mustn't be too late because my bicycle lamp isn't right, and anyway I want to wash my hair when I get back.'

Albert looked a little relieved. He had been wondering if he could afford to take Dolly to the show in the Corn Exchange put  on by the local Colored Minstrels. It might have been good fun, but they would have been late back, and Albert was not sure if his parents and Dolly's would have approved. Perhaps another time, he told himself vaguely.

'We'll have a walk in the park,' he said firmly, and called for the bill.

The daffodils were in bud, and they sat on a bench with the fish bag oozing gently beside them. Albert rested his arm along the back against Dolly's thin shoulder blades, and finding that she made no demur, shifted a little closer.

Dolly's silence stemmed from surprise rather than shyness. She did not have the heart to tell the young man that she was very uncomfortable. Albert's arm gave her a crick in the small of the back, and he was sitting heavily on the side of her skirt. Dolly doubted if the gathers would hold at the waist, as the material was rather worn. She leant a little towards him in order to minimise the strain and found Albert, much encouraged, tipping her head to rest on his shoulder.

Her discomfort now was considerable. His epaulette was stiff and dug into her cheek, and her neck was strained unbearably. A cold hairpin, sliding from her rumpled bun, lodged inside her collar and added to her troubles. Albert took her hand and held it very tightly and painfully in his own.

They sat there in silence with a chilly wind blowing round them. A bed of early wallflowers competed unsuccessfully with the damp fish bag for their attention. Dolly, squinting sideways at the daffodils, found her view impeded by Albert's neck and was interested to observe how much larger his pores were than her own. It was a decidedly clean neck, she noticed with approval, and the lobe of the only ear she could see had a healthy glow.

At last cramp began to invade her left foot, and feeling that she could bear no more, Dolly struggled into an upright position. There was a cracking sound, but whether of gathers or stiff joints Dolly could not be sure, and then the two smiled upon each other, Dolly with relief and Albert with affection.

'It's getting very cold,' said Dolly gently.

'Best be cycling home,' agreed Albert, collecting the fish bag.

They pedalled home companionably in the twilight, talking of this and that, but making no comment on their prim embrace on the park bench. Only when they stopped at Dolly's gate were future plans mentioned.

'Will you write to me sometimes when I'm away?' asked Albert, looking very young as he screwed and unscrewed Emily's bicycle bell.

'Of course I will,' said Dolly warmly.

'And come out again perhaps?' continued Albert.

'Thank you,' said Dolly, a little less warmly.

'Good,' said Albert, and looked as though he might lean across Emily's bicycle and peck her cheek. At that moment Francis Clare opened the door of the cottage.

'Got my cabbage seed, Doll?' he called cheerfully.

'Goodbye,' said Dolly hastily, 'and thank you for that lovely ice cream.'

Pushing open the gate, she trundled her bicycle towards the

house. The lamp made a pool of light round her father's familiar figure in the doorway. It was good to be home.

This incident, touching and absurd, had no real sequel, for Albert's leave ended very soon after. But Dolly kept her word and wrote occasionally telling Albert about the doings of Beech Green and Fairacre. Her letters were beautifully penned; no blots, crossings or spelling mistakes marred their exquisite pages, and their subject matter was as blameless, for Dolly had no stronger feeling than friendship for the young man and was too honest to pretend that anything more was felt. After some months the letters between them grew less and less frequent, and Dolly heard of his engagement to a girl in Colchester, some time later, with genuine pleasure and some relief.

Meanwhile, Ada's love affair gave Dolly food for thought. After his interview with the publican, Francis tried patiently to get some sense from his defiant daughter.

'I've told you and told you,' said Ada obstinately. 'We're going to get married whatever anyone says.'

'But what if he doesn't want to?' queried Francis. 'Takes two to make a marriage, and he ain't bothered to come and speak to me about it yet, has 'e?'

'Looks to me,' commented Mary, in support, 'as if you're throwing yourself at him. That's no way to go into marriage, Ada.'

'Why should he come here to be picked over and found wanting?' demanded Ada belligerently. ''Twon't do no good to either of us, as far as I can see.'

They could get no further with her in this mood. Francis was perplexed. He disliked the idea of pursuing this young man, but if he refused to come and see him then he supposed he must make some effort to find out the fellow's intentions if Ada's happiness was involved.

'Blast it, Mary!' he sighed to his wife. 'Girls is a far sight more trouble than boys when it comes to wedding 'em.'

He waited a fortnight, but nothing happened. Ada continued to see the young man, and short of locking her in her room, Francis felt he could do nothing about it. At length he went again to Caxley and had an uncomfortable session with the publican, his wife and their son.

The young man was ill at ease, but assured Francis that he wished to marry Ada. Harry Roper did not impress Francis. He was thickset, with a surly expression, and had the heavy, dark, good looks which would soon coarsen with corpulence. Francis was amazed that Ada was attracted to him.

There was no doubt, however, that she would be well provided for. Jack Roper, the publican, also had an interest in a flourishing market garden, and he proposed to set up the young couple in a small greengrocery business in the town as a wedding present. So far, he knew, Harry had failed to remain in any job for longer than a year. Marriage, and a business of his own, he hoped, would settle his son permanently. At twenty-five he should have sown all his wild oats, and it was time he turned his attention to domesticity and the raising of a family. The Ropers, for their part, liked the lively girl who seemed so determined to marry their son, and felt sure she had the power and energy to direct both her husband and the business.

The Ropers were invited to the Clares' cottage. The two families exchanged civilities, the engagement was announced, and the marriage arranged for the autumn. Mary seemed pleased with matters, but Francis had a heavy heart. It was not what he wanted for his best-loved child.

There was a triumphant excitement about Ada, throughout the weeks before the wedding, which Francis found distasteful.

'She feels she's got the better of us all,' he confided to Mary.

'But what does that matter if she's not truly happy herself? And do that young Harry really want her?'

It was Mary's turn to calm fears this time.

'Our Ada's always known what she's about, and she's chose a solid fellow as'll see she's always comfortable. He loves her all right, never you fret,' she added casually.

Francis was not completely convinced, but this matter-of-fact attitude of Mary's gave him a little comfort. Presumably women knew best in these affairs.

But when he stood beside his glowing Ada before the altar, his misgivings returned. She looked so radiant, so young and so trusting in her white lace frock, standing beside that dark stranger whom he disliked. Behind her stood Dolly, pale and demure in blue, the only bridesmaid.

Francis gave Ada away, feeling as though part of his heart had gone too, and all through the wedding breakfast, which was held in 'The Crown', he felt cold and wretched. With the rest of the party he waved goodbye to the young couple as they drove off in a carriage to the railway station, and was ashamed to find that tears blurred his final view of them.

It was Mary who remained dry-eyed.

Dolly and Emily had just finished their four years' pupil-teaching at this time. Little Miss Taylor at Fairacre School now retired, and Mr Wardle suggested that Dolly might like to carry on. She was appointed as infants' teacher that September, and continued to cycle from Beech Green daily. Emily heard of a post, some miles away at a village on the south side of Caxley, which appealed to her. An aunt lived in the village and would put her up, and she would be teaching children from twelve to fourteen, which was what she had always wanted.

The two friends, who had seen each other daily for most of their young lives, missed each other sorely. They promised to write once a week, and they met occasionally in Caxley or whenever Emily managed to get home for a week-end. Without Emily and Ada, Dolly felt quite forlorn for several weeks that autumn.

But the interests at Fairacre and its school grew more absorbing as the months passed. Mr Wardle and his wife left the village, a year after Dolly began her teaching, and a new headmaster, called Mr Hope, came to live at the school house. He was a shyer, cleverer man than his predecessor, one who loved animals and flowers, and who wrote poetry with some skill and feeling.

Dolly liked him, and his vague young wife. They had one daughter, Harriet, a child of outstanding beauty and intelligence. All three, Dolly thought, had charm and uncommon sympathy, but she missed the Wardles' splendid invigorating presence, the hearty good humour and the drive which was essential to stimulate the native laziness of the Fairacre children. She hoped that Mr Waterman's methods would not be repeated.

At first, all went well. Despite his delicate appearance and gentle ways, Mr Hope had the ability to catch the imagination of the children. He was more aware of the progress of the world than Mr Wardle had been. For Mr Wardle, Fairacre and its immediate environs offered all that was needed in interest and amusement. Mr Hope soon made his older children conscious of the exciting changes about them.

He told them about aeroplanes and the pioneers who flew them. He conjured up visions of air travel in the future for his open-mouthed, and slightly disbelieving, pupils. With a poet's flair for words he described the great icy wastes at the farthest Poles of the earth, whose mystery and beauty were just becoming known and explored by brave men. He told them of Peary and Shackleton and of Scott, and he made his country children realise that adventure was still to be found.

In advance of his time, the schoolmaster recognised the power of topical news, and photographs from the papers were pinned on the walls to encourage an interest in matters of the day. He was adroit enough, too, to relate these national events to their own small world, whenever possible, and Dolly listened to him one April morning as he pointed out the splendours of a mighty new liner.

'And Mr and Mrs Evans at Beech Green are going to sail in her,' he told them. 'When they come back I shall ask them to come and tell us all about it.'

Dolly had heard that the Evanses were going abroad from Mr Davis, who was their gardener.

'Taking poor Miss Lilian,' he said, 'to see some famous doctor over there. They say he may be able to cure her. Cuts a bit out of your brain, he does, and many a poor soul's found his wits again that way.'

Dolly thought it was brave of the Evanses, to go so far, and hoped that the proposed operation would be successful, for Miss Lilian grew more pathetic yearly, and it was common knowledge that her ageing parents feared for her future when they had gone.

A few days later Mary Clare was delighted to find a picture postcard on the mat. The postman rarely called at the little cottage, and a picture was far more exciting than a plain envelope.

She held it up for Dolly to see at the breakfast table.

'I call that real nice of Mrs Evans. Written just before they sail, she says, and she's never seen anything so lovely before. Hopes we are well, and Miss Lilian sends her regards.'

Mary put the card face upward beside the bread board and peered closely at it.

'You can see the name quite clear,' she said excitedly. '*Titanic*!'

*   *   *

Three days later the village heard the news. The names of the Evans family were not on the list of survivors. It was a stunning blow.

Mr Hope took down the picture of the ill-fated ship, but could say nothing to the children at that time. He was as stricken as they were at the horror which had come so close to them.

The house stood with its blinds drawn for three weeks. The eldest son, known to the neighbourhood as 'Mr Bertie', then moved in with his wife and young family. With him came two or three servants who had been in his employ in London.

Mr Davis gave the Clare family the news.

'There's a new chap coming to be head gardener,' he told them. 'Seems a nice enough young fellow, if you like 'em with red hair, which I don't.'

'And what's happening to you then?' enquired Francis.

'Three times a week,' said Mr Davis, 'and it suits me. Getting a bit long in the tooth these days, and the family brings us in a bit. We'll manage.'

He made his way to the door and then turned to Dolly.

'Keep your eye out for that young chap,' he said, with mock solemnity. 'You can't miss that hair. Just like a sunset it is.'

He opened the door and was gone.

CHAPTER 15

IT was strange, thought old Miss Clare, that the *Titanic* disaster in the spring of 1912 had brought such unexpected happiness in its wake.

Although, at this time, she was almost twenty-four years of

age, she had remained remarkably untouched by love. There
were several reasons for this. By nature she was reserved, and in
company she was an observer rather than a participator. Ada's
tempestuous marriage had made her cautious, and circumstances did not throw many young men across Dolly's path.
At home she found that her parents grew more dependent
upon her for company, and she herself, tired after a day's
teaching and the long cycle ride, was very content to stay at
home during the evenings.

She had not been conscious of any gap in her life. Her work,
gardening, reading, helping her mother with household
affairs and writing to Emily, kept her occupied and happy at
the cottage. She took part in the life of both villages, helping
with socials and jumble sales, fêtes and church bazaars, and
considered her life completely satisfying. She was all the more
surprised, therefore, to find how overwhelmingly easy it was
to slide into the state of love within a few weeks of Arnold
Fletcher's arrival at Beech Green.

They first met when the young man called at the cottage
with a message for Francis. Dolly was weeding, squatting down
with her back to the gate, and did not hear him approach. She
was startled by his voice, and struggled to her feet, much
hampered by an old sack which she had pinned round her for
an apron.

'You should kneel to weed,' said the young man, smiling
upon her. 'It saves your back.'

There was no doubt about who he was. The bright auburn
hair, which flamed above his pale bony face, identified him as
the Evanses' new gardener. His eyes were of that true dark
brown which is so rare in English faces, and they looked very
kindly on Dolly's discomfiture.

After that he came often. He had an easy friendliness which
disarmed Dolly immediately, and she felt happy in his com-

pany from the first. They found that they had much in common. His knowledge of plants and trees was deep, and unlike many gardeners, he was equally interested in wild growing things. He was an avid reader and a cricketer. Beech Green found him a reliable slow bowler and a swift-running fieldsman, and by the end of May he was playing regularly for the team.

Both he and Dolly enjoyed music and Arnold took great pride in a new phonograph which he sometimes brought over to the Clares' cottage. After much adjustment a hollow nasal voice echoed through the little room: 'This is an Edison Bell record,' and after a short rushing noise, the music would begin. It all seemed miraculous to the listeners, and Dolly first became acquainted with Handel and Bach, whose music she was to love throughout her life, by way of Arnold's phonograph.

It was soon common knowledge in the neighbourhood that Dolly and Arnold were 'going steady', as the villagers said. There was general approval.

'About time that girl got settled,' said Mr Davis to his wife. 'Won't have time for much of a family if she leaves it much longer.'

'Nonsense!' snorted Mrs Davis. 'Who wants to begin a family at eighteen like I did? Dolly's got plenty of sense – and plenty of time too. I shouldn't want to see her with a long string like ours.'

'But I thought you liked 'em!' answered Mr Davis, somewhat affronted by this sidelong attack.

'Case of have to!' commented his wife shortly, pushing him to one side as she bustled by with a steaming saucepan. Mr Davis wisely held his tongue. No point in adding fuel to the fire, he told himself.

Francis and Mary both seemed pleased, but Dolly sensed that her mother's approval was not whole-hearted. Latterly,

Mary's manner had been strange. She was at an age when women are the prey of moods, and Dolly had tried to be understanding. She guessed that, unconsciously, Mary clung to her last remaining child, and it was this that caused her mother to be cool at times with the young man. Nothing was ever said, and the matter was small enough to be ignored. In any case, Dolly was so deeply happy that troubles could scarcely affect her.

They became engaged later that year. Arnold took Dolly to Caxley where he bought a delicate little ring which she had seen in the jeweller's window and adored at first sight.

'But it's a *regard* ring, Dolly,' protested Arnold. 'I feel more than *regard* for you!'

But that was the ring which she wanted, and as she turned it upon her slim finger admiring the ruby, emerald, garnet, amethyst, ruby and diamond which spelt out its message, she felt that no one could be so happy.

Soon afterwards, in the Christmas holidays, Dolly paid her first visit to London, on the way to meet Arnold's parents who lived in Norwich. She had been by train from Caxley to the county town on a few occasions, but to ride to Paddington was a real adventure, and to see the capital itself an even greater thrill. Very few of the older generation in Beech Green, and not many of Dolly's, had seen London, although they lived within seventy miles of it, for fares were expensive and there were very few holidays.

She and Arnold went by horse bus from Paddington to Liverpool Street. Dolly was appalled by the number of vehicles, most of them horsedrawn, but some motor driven. The speed and dexterity with which the bicycles moved in and out of the traffic made Dolly shudder, and she found the noise worse than Caxley on a market day. The streets too seemed very dirty, and she was interested to see how necessary crossing sweepers were as they brushed a clear way across the road for the ladies to use.

Dolly had never seen anything so enthralling as the ladies' fashions in Oxford Street. She admired the wide hats tied on with veiling, the net necklets held up with whalebone which gave their wearers a haughty appearance, and the long sweeping skirts, held gracefully to keep them from the dirt, above neat buttoned boots. The journey to Liverpool Street passed all too quickly.

She was glad of Arnold's protection in that cavernous place of reeking smoke, hooting engines and hustling people, but once the sad poverty of the slums was passed she settled back to enjoy the different scenery of East Anglia. She never forgot her first sight of those wide wind-swept heaths and the magnificent avenues of the Norfolk countryside, with great clouds bowling in from the North Sea, moving like pillars of snow across the vast blue sky.

Arnold's parents were welcoming. They lived in a small crooked road in the shadow of the ancient cathedral. Dolly liked them at once, and was taken on a tour of relatives who lived in the city, and who proved equally friendly. She and Arnold spent three happy days in Norwich, and she grew to love the place more with every hour that passed.

When the time came to return to Beech Green, and the farewells were over, she stood at the train window and watched with regret the last of that lovely and lively city slide behind her.

Arnold, amused at her pensive face, put his arm round her comfortingly.

'We'll come again,' he promised. 'Lots of times.'

But Dolly never saw Norwich again.

Long engagements were common in those days, and Dolly felt no hardship in waiting for her wedding. It was an idyllic time, she thought. She saved as much as she could from her small salary, and bought and made many things for her future home. Friends presented her with linen and china, and Dolly found much satisfaction in her well-filled bottom drawer.

Emily, who was also engaged, to the son of a local farmer, was as busy and as happy as her friend. The two girls had plenty to talk about now when they met, and despite the major distraction of their future husbands, the weekly letters still passed between them. There were things, Dolly discovered, that one could only tell to Emily, no matter how dear Arnold might be, and their shared school experiences made a constant bond.

Fairacre School had its problems at this time which perturbed Dolly. In the January following her visit to Norwich, a tragedy had occurred in the headmaster's house.

Harriet Hope, the only child, had died from the same disease which had taken little Frank Clare. She had been a child of such unusual vivacity and beauty that the blow was all the more cruel. Mr Hope and his wife could not face the village for a week after the funeral, and Dolly coped alone with both classes, glad of the extra work and responsibility which kept her from dwelling on the loss of the attractive child.

When at last Mr Hope returned, he was a changed man. His vigour had gone, never to return, and his duties were undertaken mechanically. Worse still, he began drinking heavily, and frequently arrived in the schoolroom smelling strongly of liquor. It was not long before he began to make an excuse to leave the school soon after ten each morning, and could be seen making his way to 'The Beetle and Wedge'. He returned within half an hour just in time to mark the arithmetic he had set before his departure. But his marking pencil often wavered, and the smell of beer was most noticeable. It was small wonder that the older boys and girls winked and giggled at each other behind his back, and that the parents at Fairacre, torn between pity and indignation, wondered if they should report their schoolmaster to those in authority.

While Mr Hope was out, the door in the partition between the two classrooms was left open so that Dolly could keep an eye on both classes. She took to setting her babies some quiet work in their little desks, for during the headmaster's absence she knew she would have to make several visits to his room. Through the open door she caught glimpses of mischievous dumb show. One wag would pretend to swig from a bottle, another would clutch his stomach and roll his eyes in mock drunkenness, and these capers aroused titters from the rest of the children. It was a difficult time for Dolly, and she found it better to forestall this insolence rather than deal with its effects. Her presence in the room guaranteed good behaviour, for most of the children had been in her hands only a year or two before, and young though she was, Dolly's tall dignity commanded respect.

The babies suspected nothing, and were content to set out their counters and attempt the simple adding up and taking away sums displayed on the blackboard in Miss Clare's clear hand. Sometimes, during those quiet periods when she walked the length of Fairacre School with all its young scholars in her care, Dolly grieved for the tragedy which was being enacted around her.

Standing at the narrow Gothic window, she gazed at the dazzle of fruit blossom in the school garden, and the grandeur of the elms against the sky. She could see the roofs of the village, the blue smoke spiralling against the background of the distant downs, as blue as the smoke itself. It was appalling to think that a man could throw away such beauty and the security of a home and congenial work for the sake of drink.

That sorrow had driven him to it, Dolly knew well. That same sorrow had broken his wife's health and this added to his own misery. But Dolly could not understand why he gave way. He had so much to lose, and to her mind, there was so much around him to offer comfort and sanity. The countryside alone offered untold blessings of sight, sound and scent. He had the affection and, till recently, the respect of the children and their parents, and a fine gift of teaching. His conduct was incomprehensible to young Dolly.

What Dolly failed to recognise, because of her inexperience, was that she judged Mr Hope by her own standards. She had a calm wisdom beyond her years, and the ability to stand aside from a problem and assess it rationally. No matter how troubled her heart might be, as it was at the unaccountable attack on her by 'the marsh' boy so many years before, or by the death of Frank or by Ada's sudden vituperation, yet her head took command and dictated the course to take through stormy waters. That a man might be engulfed by the storms, and finally ship-wrecked, simply through lack of judgement, was a state of affairs which Dolly could not imagine.

Nor could she realise the state of despair to which a man might be driven so that he was impervious to the world around him. Dolly's quick eye and ear supplied her constantly with a succession of small delights – a field of buttercups, a child playing with an animal, the bubbling of a clear spring in the hedge, the flaming of Arnold's hair in the sunshine. That a man might be stricken deaf and blind with grief, and so be cut off from the mercies of nature's healing, was beyond the girl's understanding, at this time.

After some unhappy months, matters improved a little, for the morning absences ceased and Mr Hope remained on duty. It was common knowledge that the vicar, who was chairman of the managers of the school, called upon the headmaster one evening and remained in his house for nearly three hours. After this warning, 'The Beetle and Wedge' saw Mr Hope no more, but he did not stop drinking. He and his wife went out less and less in the evenings. Failing health, and shame at her husband's condition, kept Mrs Hope house-bound, while despair drove Mr Hope to the bottle, which led only to further despair.

So the sad state of affairs drifted on, and it was lucky that Dolly had so much happiness in her love for Arnold and in the bright world around her that she was able to work by the side of the pathetic headmaster of Fairacre School with constant cheerfulness.

An added joy, in the early summer of 1914, was the birth of Ada's first child. Despite her robust good health, Ada and her husband had waited six years for a son, and three miscarriages made them wonder if they were doomed to have no family.

Dolly and Arnold went to Caxley one evening to see the new baby. Harry Roper let them in the door by the side of his shop. The greengrocery business was doing well and, as his father had hoped, Harry had settled down well with his young wife. It was quite apparent, though, that in spite of her youth Ada ruled her husband. It was she who urged him to buy a smart horse and cart and to employ a good-looking young man to drive it on a round. Harry would have been content to let customers come to him. Ada saw that 'H. Roper – Caxley's Finest Greengrocer' went further afield.

Dolly suspected that it was not a very happy marriage. Prosperity had thickened their figures and lined their brows. Harry's native indolence needed to be scourged by Ada's nagging tongue. Material success meant the vindication of her early rebellion to Ada, and she intended to show the world that the Ropers had succeeded. It was an attitude which jarred on the unworldly Dolly, but on this May evening she rejoiced that her sister and brother-in-law should have a new and unifying interest.

Ada lay in a vast brass bedstead, her son in a beribboned cradle at her side. Dolly had never seen her look so pretty.

'Well, there's your nephew,' said Ada, nodding to the swaddled infant. 'And your godson, too, if you like the idea.'

Dolly was much moved. She picked up the warm bundle and looked at the tiny crumpled face among the shawls. It was more than she had ever hoped for, and it meant a new and happier relationship with Ada which she welcomed gladly.

'There's nothing I'd like more, Ada,' she said softly. The two sisters looked at each other with a sympathy and affection which had been lacking for years. It was as though they were children again, sharing the joy of a precious new present.

'We're going to call him "John" after Harry's dad,' said Ada, at last. 'And "Francis" after our dad. We'll have him christened at Beech Green when I'm up and about.'

It sounded perfect, Dolly told her. She returned the sleeping baby to its cradle, kissed Ada with warmth, and made her farewells.

Arnold, cycling home beside her, noted his Dolly's glowing looks and attributed her happiness to the new nephew. It was good to be looking forward to their own marriage later this year, he thought, for Dolly was now twenty-six and it was time they began a family of their own.

But Dolly's thoughts were of the past rather than the future. In those few minutes with Ada it seemed that some of the comradeship of their childhood had been regained. In the long look which had passed between them, Dolly recognised the old Ada she had always loved, and believed that that brief vision was a happy augury for the future.

CHAPTER 16

THE marriages of Dolly Clare and Emily Davis were planned for the autumn. There were practical country reasons for this, for Edgar, Emily's young man, would have helped his father to get in the harvest by that time, and could be spared for a few days for the less important job of marrying and taking a short honeymoon.

Arnold, too, would be particularly busy in the Evanses' garden in September, and the cottage promised them by Mr

Bertie would not be vacated until Michaelmas Day. He had promised to get the decoration and repairs done immediately, and the young couple expected to be able to live in their first home towards the end of October.

Dolly was so engrossed with household plans and the making of her trousseau that she took little notice of the newspapers and the talk of troubles abroad. She was vaguely aware that a foreign Archduke, with the same name as her father's, had been shot, in a country whose name meant nothing to her. She heard her father talking to a friend about it in the garden one hot June evening, but she was bent double, with her hands thrust among the thorns and fruit of the gooseberry bushes, and her attention was otherwise engaged. This would be the last time, she told herself, that she would pick the crop to bottle for her mother. Next year she would be picking in the Evanses' garden and the fruit jars would stand upon her own white shelves.

All through July, as Dolly spent her last few weeks at Fairacre School, trouble brewed far away. She heard Mr Hope talking to the boys and girls about Germany and her military power. At home Arnold and her father shook their heads, and the names of Sir Ernest Grey and the Czar of Russia and the Kaiser and Crown Prince flew back and forth across the room. Dolly was too happy to worry about such far-off affairs, and it was not until the first day of August that Dolly realised that her own small world might well be shattered by a great explosion outside. It seemed, suddenly, that everyone spoke of Belgium – Belgium's neutrality, Belgium being overrun by the Germans, Belgium who must be helped.

'We wouldn't go to *war*, would we?' asked Dolly, much shocked, one Sunday morning. Arnold had cycled to Caxley for a paper, and it was spread out upon the table with all four grouped around it. The headlines said 'Germany declares war on Russia', and on the same page were the words 'Bank rate rises to 10 per cent.' It all seemed incomprehensible to Dolly, but from the gravity of the men's expressions she realised that calamity was threatening.

'It'll be France next,' said Arnold quietly. 'And we'll have to go in.'

'That be blowed,' answered Francis robustly. For him still the French were the enemy. Hadn't his mother told him Bony would get him when he was a boy, even though the Frenchman had been dead for years? Tradition dies slowly in the country, and the idea of spilling his blood for a parcel of Frenchies did not suit Francis Clare.

'And what about Belgium then?' asked Arnold.

'Oh well,' said Francis roundly, 'that's a different kettle o' fish. If the Kaiser steps in there, he's for it.'

'Comes to the same thing,' said Arnold laconically.

In two days' time Arnold's words were proved true, and Dolly, with mounting horror, watched the enthusiasm which greeted Britain's entry into the war. Just as, faced with Mr Hope's tragedy, she deplored his rejection of reason, so now in this world-wide dilemma she was appalled to think that no settlement could be reached between nations except by the idiocy of war. She tried to talk about it to her mother, but Mary shrugged her shoulders, and dismissed the subject with:

'It's the men, dear! They govern the country, and they knows what's best.'

When Dolly retorted that it was a pity they did govern then, if that was what they thought best, she was teased by her father and Arnold.

'Our Dolly's turning Suffragette! Votes for women!' they cried. And Dolly smiled and remained silent, for she knew it was useless to try to explain the fire, kindled by injustice and deep feeling, which burnt within her.

The summer holidays had begun and Dolly had time to

think of things. She had planned to return and teach for a few weeks in the autumn term before getting married. On marriage she was obliged to give up her post, for no married women teachers were employed in that area. She was looking forward to earning a little more money before her enforced resignation, to put towards the many expenses of their new home.

Now these long-settled plans were thrown into confusion. Within a week of the declaration of war, Mr Bertie, who was in the Army Reserve, left to join his regiment, and his wife announced that the house would be turned into a hospital. She explained to Arnold that his cottage would be available if he should need it in October, but it was quite clear that she imagined that he too would be in the Army by that time. In this she was right.

Dolly and Arnold discussed their future long and earnestly. Lord Kitchener's appeal for half a million men had gone out, and Arnold was determined to become one of Kitchener's Army without delay. Dolly, though sad at heart, could not help admiring his single-mindedness. He looked upon the war as a great adventure, and something more – a crusade against the evils of subjection. She did all in her power to make his going easier. It would have been wrong, and also impossible, to deflect him from his purpose.

At first, immediate marriage seemed the right thing, but after some cooler thoughts they decided against it.

'It's best if you carry on with your teaching,' said Arnold, 'while I'm away. Something to stop you from fretting. We'll get married a bit later, say, after Christmas. It'll all be over by then, they say, and we can settle down without parting.'

It seemed sensible, and Dolly agreed. After all, it was only a few months, and maybe Arnold would worry less about her if she were still under her parents' care. Sadly and bravely, the young couple rearranged their lives, and neither spoke of the possibility of mutilation or death, for it barely entered their thoughts.

The next day Arnold and a dozen other young men drove into Caxley to the recruiting centre. Dolly never forgot that summer morning. Harold Miller, son to the man who had let Francis have the cottage so long ago, held the reins at the front of one of his own farm waggons. He was a lusty red-faced man in his thirties, grinning broadly on this unforgettable morning, and thoroughly enjoying the thought of excitement ahead.

The waggon was freshly painted bright blue, with red wheels. Two massive black carthorses pulled it, their coats shining like coal and the brasswork of their harness jingling and gleaming in the sunlight. Two small Union Jacks fluttered from the front of the waggon, and Harold Miller had decorated his whip with red, white and blue ribbons that fluttered in the breeze. It was a brave, gay turn-out, which matched the spirits of the young men riding aloft, and the villagers waved enthusiastically when it descended the long slope of the downs and stopped at Beech Green to collect the recruits.

They were all dressed in their Sunday suits. White collars, or clean white mufflers, showed up the sunburnt country faces, and Dolly thought that they looked as fine a body of men as any in England. They glowed with good health and eagerness. Normally as quiet and docile as the powerful horses in front of them, the thrill of war had woken them to life. Ahead lay adventure, the unknown, hazards to face and battles to win. Now they would see, as such lucky chaps as Albert Davis had seen, foreign parts and foreign ways. They would exchange the confines of home for a limitless new world, and at the heart of each of them lay the encouraging certainty that they were fighting for a right and proper cause.

Dolly, with a pang, thought that Arnold had never looked so happy as at that moment. His red hair glowed above his sun-tanned face. He had one arm round his neighbour's shoulders, as the great waggon rumbled away from the waving crowd, and looked as though he were one of a band of brothers, each as exulting and purposeful as he was himself. She remembered old Mr Davis's words so long ago. No woman could ever know completely the whole of a man's heart.

All through August, Dolly and her mother went several times a week to Caxley Station to help to distribute cups of tea and sandwiches to the troops, who passed through in their thousands to Southampton. Thanks to the British Fleet, the Expeditionary Force was ferried safely across to France in the ten days between August 7th and 17th. Dolly was told that this meant that a hundred and sixty thousand men were carried during that time, and sometimes, it seemed to her, the majority must have come through Caxley Station.

Hot and tired, she cut bread and butter, sliced meat, mixed mustard, tended urns and milk jugs, and carried trays up and down the length of the packed trains in the broiling heat. But she forgot her minor discomforts in the warmth of the welcome she was given by the men. Most of them had been travelling for many hours, but their spirits were as unquenchable as their thirst. To Dolly they looked unbelievably young in their khaki uniform, and had the same air of gaiety that Arnold wore. She waved to each departing train, a long, long monster fluttering with a thousand hands, until it disappeared round the line which curved southward to the sea. Then she hurried back to the trestle tables to prepare for the next train load which would follow so soon after.

Emily helped too, and sometimes Ada left her baby, and spent an afternoon at the station. Harry had also volunteered for service and was now busy putting the shop into order, before he was called up, so that Ada could run it easily in his absence. Arnold, and the others who had jolted to Caxley in the waggon, awaited their call-up impatiently, carrying on with their jobs in a fever of suspense. Suppose it should all be over before they arrived?

They did not have long to wait. As news of the retreat from Mons came through at the end of August, Arnold and his friends were sent to a training camp in Dorset.

'It won't be for long,' Arnold promised her as they said good bye. 'You look out for a nice little house for us to go to after Christmas. We'll have the Kaiser squashed by then.'

He echoed the general feeling of optimism. Despite the ugly sound of the retreat from Mons, it was only a set-back, people told each other, and a chance to prepare for a resounding blow at the enemy. Britain was the greatest country in the world, supported by the mightiest Empire ever known – it was unthinkable that such power could be beaten. Francis and Mary, and many like them, remembering the display of might at Queen Victoria's jubilee, could see no possibility of defeat at the hands of mere foreigners. Dolly had private doubts, but was glad of the robust spirit around her.

At the end of November Arnold had a short leave before going to the Western Front. He was thinner than before, but his face glowed with health and high spirits. He was more gentle and loving than Dolly had ever known him, refused to let her show any hint of sadness, and forbade her to accompany him to Caxley Station on the evening of his return.

She walked slowly with him, in the early twilight, along the road to Caxley, and they stopped beneath a sycamore tree to make their farewells. The bare branches seemed to stretch kindly arms above them, as if in blessing, and at their feet the winged seeds lay on the wet road, a sign of hope and life ahead.

He put a little packet into her hand before taking her in his arms. It was only then, and for a brief moment, that Dolly

caught a glimpse of something more than resolute gaiety in his
mien. For that one telling second, darkness came into his eyes,
a weary hopelessness shadowed his face, as though he knew
that he was powerless in the grip of the fates.

Their faces were cold as they kissed, and Dolly's throat ached
with the effort of controlling her tears. But when they finally
parted Arnold's smile was as warm as ever. He took his cap
from his head at the bend of the lane and waved it cheerfully.
His fiery head shone with the same bronze glow as the winter
sun's slipping below the shoulder of the downs behind him.

When he disappeared from view, Dolly sank on to the
damp bank among the writhing roots of the old tree, and let
the hot tears fall. She made no sound, but sat hunched silently,
tasting the salt drops as they ran over her mouth.

When at last it was dark, she rose to her feet, patting the comforting rough bark of the tree which had witnessed her grief. She never passed it again without remembering that evening.

In the quietness of her bedroom she undid the packet. It contained an oval locket made of gold threaded on a long gold chain. Inside was a photograph of Arnold, and facing it, a lock of his blazing hair.

She slipped the chain over her throbbing head, and by the wavering light of the candle, surveyed her blotched swollen face and the beauty of the locket which lay cold upon her breast. She was to wear it every day of her long life.

One February day of biting cold, Dolly returned home from school to find an incoherent letter from Arnold's parents, written on a flimsy half sheet of paper, with the ink blurred by tears. He had been killed by a hand grenade lobbed into his water-logged trench near the Ypres Canal. Three other men had been killed instantly with him.

Dolly's first reaction was of stubborn disbelief. A flame as vital as Arnold's could not be snuffed out so easily. It was all a dreadful mistake. Why, she had had a letter from him only yesterday! She pushed the paper, almost impatiently, towards her mother.

It was Mary's anguished face which really convinced Dolly that the news was true, and later still the rare embrace of her sympathetic father. But for many days she was too numbed to cry. It was as though this tragedy had happened to someone else. She went, pale and dazed, about her daily life. She set work for the children, read them stories, bound up their broken knees and listened to their tales. Francis and Mary, Mr Hope, and all who knew her in Beech Green and Fairacre feared for her reason. There was an icy remoteness about her which frightened them into silence when she approached.

Even Emily had no power to thaw her. During those dark weeks she came daily to the Clares' cottage to do her best to comfort her friend.

'There's nothing you can do for me,' Dolly told her gently. 'Don't be sorry for me. I don't feel anything at all.' She was touched by Emily's staunch devotion and felt almost guilty that she should be so calm.

'Sometimes I think,' she told Emily one day, 'that my heart was killed at the same time as Arnold. Only my poor dull head works now.'

It was a small incident a week or two later that snapped Dolly's chains and released her grief. Every morning she fed the birds which came to the doorstep of the cottage. Among them was a robin, bolder than the rest, who came so frequently that the Clares' cat ignored it. But on this particular morning the cat, who had been watching the proceedings from a window-sill, leapt suddenly upon the robin, killing it at a blow, and returned immediately to the window-sill where it yawned indolently.

Dolly was shaken with fury at this wanton attack. This robin had been hatched in the damson tree in the garden. She had watched its parents, day after day, feeding their young. Their efforts had brought up the little family, all of whom had gone, except for this one. The Clares had thrown him crumbs daily, and Francis looked for his company when he dug in the garden. His clear piping and bright eye had cheered the wretched winter.

That such abundant vitality should turn to half an ounce of dead feathers, with the stroke of a paw, was horrifying to Dolly. Tears of pity and rage shook her as she lifted the victim. Its breast was the same colour as the hair within her locket, and it was this that made her tears fall faster. Now the full realisation of her loss gripped her. A blow as cruel and as senseless as the cat's had robbed Arnold of life and her of joy. The paroxysms of grief continued unabated all that day, to be succeeded by a week of such black and hopeless despair that Dolly longed to die.

Only then did she understand the pitiful state of those who could find no comfort. She could understand now the depths of Mr Hope's despair, his rejection of a world which could offer him no solace. Never again, in her young arrogance, would she despise those who failed to interest themselves in the bright world about them. There was no bright world for those in the pit.

It was a long time before Dolly herself could clamber slowly from it and seek the light again.

CHAPTER 17

THE war ground on mercilessly. Now there was a grimmer spirit everywhere, for it was obvious that victory would not be easily won. Fighting was going on in all quarters of the globe, but it was the losses on the western front that meant most to the people of Fairacre and Beech Green, for it was there that almost all their men were fighting.

In April 1915, while Dolly still groped her way to normality, the new weapon of gas was used at Ypres, where Arnold's broken body shared a grave with ten others.

Dolly never forgot the horror with which she heard this news. It was followed almost immediately by a message from Emily's Edgar, who was out there.

Dolly was with her when his postcard arrived. It said starkly: 'I beg you to send me a gas mask.' Bewildered and shocked, the two girls looked dumbly at each other. What was a gas mask? Where could you buy one? How could you make one?

With no time to lose they fashioned a thick pad of cotton wool which they bound with tape, adding more tapes to tie it round the head. They tried it on each other, and in normal times would have laughed at the ludicrous sight. But it was too gruesome an affair this time for laughter.

They packed it up, with a hasty loving note from Emily, and Dolly and she cycled to Caxley to catch the last post. The lanes and fields were brushed with tender green, and the downs, ineffably peaceful, brooded over all. It seemed unbelievable to Dolly that, within hours, the parcel they carried so carefully would be in another world where there were no trees left, no birds to sing, but only grey mud, guns, and suffering men.

It was gas which ended Edgar's war service. At the end of May he returned to England, a gasping, coughing shadow, and was sent to a hospital on the south coast. For months Emily made the long anxious journey each week while the young man struggled back to life. It was now Dolly's turn to be of comfort, and she marvelled at the endurance of Emily's slight frame and the light of courage that shone in her clear grey eyes. Although she taught all the week at Springbourne, where she was now headmistress, and worked increasingly hard at home, she still undertook the week-end journeys with unfailing hope.

Dolly, at Fairacre school, thought how little the war had changed it. Unlike Springbourne, its headmaster had not gone to war. Mr Hope's repeated attempts to join up met with failure through ill-health. He could best serve his country by staying at his post, he was told. He grew shakier and more morose as time went on, and the morning visits to 'The

Beetle and Wedge' were resumed. Dolly could not help hearing the gossip that flew about the village, though she herself preserved silence, steadfastly refusing to be drawn into discussions about her headmaster.

Two evenings a week she stayed late at the school with a party of local Red Cross workers. They sewed, knitted and packed parcels under the lamps swinging from the lofty roof, while the news of husbands and brothers and sons far away was exchanged. The women were extra kind to Dolly at this time. Her tragedy touched them, and they felt great admiration for her increasing care of the children.

'Carries that school along alone these days,' commented one. 'She's the one that should be head there.'

'They don't learn much after they've left Miss Clare,' agreed another.

Certainly Dolly had enough to do. The school was growing. A family of Belgian refugees contributed five more children, and there were several Londoners who had been sent to stay with local relatives to escape the bombing attacks on the capital. Dolly enjoyed their fresh outlook, and, remembering her own apprehension as a newcomer to Fairacre school, tried to make them particularly welcome.

Now that so many men were away, far more women went out to work. A munitions factory on the outskirts of Caxley employed a number of Fairacre mothers, and Dolly passed them each morning as they cycled into work. To her mind, they looked happier and healthier cycling along together in all weathers, than they had when they were cooped up in their cottages. Many of them were tasting independence, and the pleasure of earning, for the first time in their lives. This emancipation would not be lightly thrown away when the war was over.

The food shortage, which so seriously affected the towns,

was not apparent at Beech Green and Fairacre. Dolly was made
aware of their good fortune one day when she was throwing
maize to the chickens in Mr Hope's garden. A boy from London watched in amazement.

'We 'ad that for dinner up London,' he told her disap-
provingly. 'My mum'd give you what for if she saw you doin'
that.'

Dolly realised that the rebuke was a just one. Certainly they
were short of such things as sugar and sweets, but corn,
vegetables, fruit, and even butter, were plentiful in the quiet
little world of Fairacre. They had much to be thankful for,
thought Dolly, beginning once more to find comfort in the
work she loved, and the ever changing natural beauty about
her.

Life could never be quite as sweet again. A vital part of
her had died, it seemed, with Arnold's going; a part which
beauty, work or the love of friends could not replace. But from
these sources came a measure of comfort for which she was
humbly grateful. She learnt, at this time, the invaluable lesson
of finding happiness in little things, and by picking up small
crumbs of comfort as she went about her daily work nursed
her damaged spirit back to health.

In the summer of 1916 Dolly was looking forward to
Emily's wedding. Edgar was still an invalid, at a convalescent
home not far from his first hospital. Emily made her week-
end journeys regularly, and the plans for the long-awaited
marriage were all ready. One of the farm cottages was waiting
for them, and Edgar was expected to return to light duties on
the farm at Michaelmas time.

The two young women spent many evenings together
making curtains and covers for the new house. Dolly's pleasure
in the preparations was occasionally clouded by her own sense
of loss, but she was careful never to let Emily know her feelings.

She was sincerely glad for her friend, she was fond of Edgar, and looked forward to being a frequent visitor to the little home when they had settled in.

One sunny evening she had arranged to meet Emily at the empty cottage to help her measure the floors for lino and rugs. Edgar's farm lay beyond Springbourne, in a wide valley, hidden by the swell of the downs from the villages of Beech Green and Fairacre, and hard by the larger farm of Harold Miller. As Dolly Clare pushed her bicycle up the steep chalky path from Beech Green she thought of the varying fates which war had brought to the men of that district. While Arnold lay dead, and Edgar broken, Harold Miller went from strength to strength, and had just been commissioned on the field, she heard, at Thiepval. He would be a gallant fighter, she felt sure, remembering his tough smiling face as she had seen it last as he drove his comrades to Caxley in the brightly painted farm waggon. How many more would come back with just such honours, she wondered? And how many would share Edgar's and Arnold's fate? Accompanied by such pensive thoughts, she rode down the other side of the downs and made her way to the cottage.

The door was open, but there was no welcoming cry from Emily. Dolly stepped in and saw her sitting, dazed, upon a wide window-sill. In silence Emily handed her a letter. Dolly read it slowly in a shaft of evening sunshine which fell through the little window. The only sounds were the fluttering of a butterfly against the pane and the distant bleat of sheep on Edgar's farm. It said:

Dear Em,

    I don't know how to tell you. I don't expect you to forgive me. But I can't marry you. There is a nurse here who looked after me all the time. I love her very much and

we are getting married as soon as we can. I have tried to tell
you before, but never managed it.

Em, I am sorry, but you will meet someone much better
than me. I don't deserve you anyway.

Your loving,

Edgar.

Stunned, Dolly slid on to the window-sill beside her friend
and put her arms round her. She held Emily's head against her
shoulder. They sat in dreadful silence, while Emily's slight
frame shook with sobs, and her tears made a warm wet patch
on Dolly's print blouse.

After a time, Emily straightened up and looked dazedly
about the room. She folded the letter carefully, tucked it into
her wide belt, and stood up. She dried her eyes, smoothed her
hair, and went from the empty room through the front door.

Dolly followed her, torn with grief and fearful for her wel-
fare. The evening sun had turned everything to gold, and
glinted on the key in Emily's hand.

Dolly watched her close the door of the house which was to
have been her home. She turned the key resolutely in the lock
and thrust it, with the letter, into her belt. Then she looked
steadily at her friend. Her clear grey eyes were swollen with
crying, but were as brave as ever. They lit with sympathy as
they observed Dolly's stricken state, and she came to her
friend and kissed her soundly.

'It's her house now,' she said firmly. 'Edgar's made his
choice. I'll abide by it.'

Without a backward glance she mounted her bicycle and
the two friends rode slowly, and with heavy hearts, back to
Beech Green.

Dolly often thought, later, that Emily's lot was far harder than

her own. She was fated to live for the rest of her life within a mile
or two of Edgar and his wife, cloaking her feelings before all
who knew the sad story. Public knowledge of one's affairs is a
factor of village life which can cause annoyance. Sometimes it
can cause tragedy, but sometimes it can be a source of strength.
The sympathy which flowed to Emily, as a result of Edgar's
marriage to another, did not show itself in words, but she was
conscious of much kindness and was grateful for it.

Dolly never forgot Emily's reaction to this blow, and the
turning of the key upon her hopes with such swift resolution.
She had come to terms with the situation as decisively as she
had so many years ago, when she had heard of Queen Victoria's death and saw in it a comfort to little Frank Clare, in a
world unknown. It was her acceptance of fate, which Dolly
admired. She seemed to bear no rancour towards Edgar, and
refused to discuss his future wife.

'What use would it be,' she said one day to Dolly, 'to try and
hold Edgar against his will? I don't want a marriage like that.'

But not many women, Dolly thought, would have felt that
way. Some people wondered if Emily Davis were heartless,
and if her love for Edgar had waned during the long months of
waiting. But Dolly knew it was otherwise.

In the years that followed, Emily never passed the house that
might have been her own, if she could help it. She would walk
a mile further, along a winding lane, rather than take the steep
path beside the cottage, and when, by chance, she and Dolly
came across Edgar one day, resting beneath the sycamore tree
where she had said good-bye to Arnold, Emily's sudden pallor
told more than words, and the look in her eyes reminded Dolly
of the stricken gaze of some dying animal. As she knew only
too well, time would bring merciful relief from pain, but it
would never cure the cause.

*   *   *

The visits of Ada and her children did much to cheer them all at this time. John Francis, Dolly's godchild, was a rampageous two-year-old when his sister was born, and Mary and Francis were the most indulgent grandparents.

Ada drove over in a smart governess cart from Caxley whenever she could spare time from the business. Harry seemed to be enjoying the war. He was fighting in Italy, and wrote cheerful letters home about the lovely country, promising to bring Ada there for a holiday when the war was over. His opinion of his Austrian enemies was low, and of his Italian comrades in arms not much higher, but he gave Ada to understand that Harry Roper was equal to coping with all difficulties. In truth, Harry quite liked his freedom again. His naturally buoyant spirits had been kept in check by Ada who had seen that any excess energy was harnessed to the business. Now he had a free rein, and Harry was to look upon his years with the army as one of the happiest times of his life.

Ada was now a very prosperous matron. Dolly marvelled at her extensive wardrobe, the children's expensive toys and the lavish amount of food which she generously brought to her parents' cottage.

Francis gloried in his Ada's success. Mary seemed less enthusiastic. It was the children that roused her spirits. It seemed as if she became young again when they tumbled about the cottage floor or called from the garden.

For all Ada's ostentation and finery, which jarred upon Dolly, yet she was warmly welcome. Despite the differences in temperament, the two sisters were fond of each other, and the children were a strong uniting bond. Harry's absence meant that the family saw more of one another. It was a comfort to Dolly to share the responsibility of her parents' care, and she hoped that Harry's homecoming would not sever the ties which had grown stronger during the war years.

At the beginning of November 1918, a jubilant letter came from Harry Roper describing the taking of an island called Grave di Papadopoli in the middle of the river Piave. He had helped to build bridges over which the Italians poured to victory, splitting the Austrian army in two.

'Now the way's wide open,' wrote Harry exultantly. 'With Austria down in the mud, we make straight for Berlin!'

The war news from all quarters was as cheering as Harry's. Mutiny had broken out in the German Fleet at Kiel, the Americans had cut the German eastern and western forces by taking Sedan, and the Allies were pursuing the enemy on the Meuse. The news that Foch was meeting German delegates, to arrange an armistice, sent the hopes of everyone soaring. On November 11, Harry Miller of Beech Green, with five other local men, entered Mons with the victorious British army, while the bells of that shattered town played 'Tipperary.' Early on the same morning the Armistice was signed, and fighting ended at 11 a.m.

In Caxley the rumours flew round that Monday morning. Someone said that the news had been telephoned to the Post Office. Flags began to appear on buildings and the bell ringers hurried to the parish church. But no official confirmation was forthcoming, and it was decided to wait a little longer. The market place and High Street began to fill with excited crowds.

At half past twelve official confirmation of the Armistice was posted in Caxley Post Office and the town's suspense was over. The bells pealed out, the Union Jack was hoisted on the Town Hall and flags of all nations sprouted from roofs and windows. Monday's meagre war-time ration of cold meat was ignored while Caxley rejoiced.

At Fairacre Dolly heard the news from Mr Hope, during the afternoon. One of the children had brought a collection of

French and Belgian postcards to show her. His father had sent
them regularly – beautiful objects of silk with fine embroidery
showing flowers and crossed flags of the Allies. Dolly was
holding them in her hand when Mr Hope burst into the room.

'It's over!' he cried, his face alight. 'The war's over!'

The babies looked at him in amazement. They remembered
no other kind of life. War had always been their background.
His excitement was incomprehensible to them.

He called the school to attention, told them the news and
then gave a prayer of thanksgiving. School ended early that
day, and Dolly rode home through the grey November
afternoon with much to think about. Rejoicing, for her, was
tempered by Arnold's loss, but she felt overwhelming relief
at the ending of suffering and slaughter.

Now the sons and lovers, the husbands and fathers, would
come home again, and the village would have young men to
work in the fields and to laugh in the lanes. Now the girls and
wives and mothers would find happiness, glad to have someone to share the joyful responsibilities of home life.

But not all. How many cottage homes, Dolly wondered,
mourned today when all the world was gay with flags and
bells?

Over forty years later, old Miss Clare felt her eyelids
pricking at the memory of that distant day. She knew now the
price that the parish of Beech Green had paid.

Twenty-six names were carved at the foot of the stone war
memorial, now weathered to a gentle grey. In the neighbouring parish of Fairacre seventeen young men had died, so that
over forty men had been taken from the thousand people who
made up the population of the two parishes. Miss Clare had
known them all, and could never be reconciled to their loss.
She honoured the high ideals of sacrifice and patriotism which

had illumined the path of these young men, but the tragic pity of it all overcame her other feelings.

In the years that followed, poetry became a source of joy and comfort to Miss Clare, but the loveliest songs sung by the young war poets who were her contemporaries, moved her so swiftly to weeping that she could not bring herself to read them often. 'The heartbreak at the heart of things', as one of them wrote, was too poignant for Miss Clare's generation ever to forget.

In the heat of the June sunshine Miss Clare's old fingers strayed to the locket. She bent her white head to look at it. It was thin and smooth with years of wear, and its glitter had mellowed to a soft golden sheen. But inside, the dear face of Arnold Fletcher was still clear and unlined, and his bright hair had no touch of grey. For Arnold and his comrades would never grow old.

CHAPTER 18

OUTWARDLY, Beech Green and Fairacre seemed to change little in the years after the war. Two bungalows were built on the road between the two villages, but no other new houses for some time. Most of the men returned to the villages, but some, unsettled by the last few years, took this chance of leaving the country and moving townwards.

Harold Miller was now in charge of the farm at Springbourne, as his old father had died during the war. He found himself so short of men that he decided to sell several of his outlying cottages, including the Clares'. Francis was given the first chance to buy it for the sum of two hundred pounds. The family spent several evenings in earnest discussion, and finally decided to purchase it with the savings of a lifetime.

'Well, I never thought to live in a house of my own,' declared Mary proudly. 'Now we don't need to fret about paying the rent every week.'

'It's to be yours when we're gone,' said Francis to Dolly. 'Ada's well provided for, and this place don't mean much to her, and never did.'

He looked through the leaded panes at the trim garden, and Dolly saw the pride of possession light up his face.

'And if you was hard pressed,' he continued, 'you could always sell it. Or say you got married,' he added, somewhat doubtfully.

'We don't need to think about that for a good few years,' replied Dolly. 'You'll enjoy it for another twenty or thirty.'

Ada and Harry bought a house about the same time. Living over the shop, Ada said, was downright common, and if they didn't have a place on the hill on the south side of Caxley, like all the other people who had done well, their two children would never be able to hold up their heads. Harry, delighted to be back and to find a flourishing business and money in the bank, agreed readily. Within a year they were installed in a brand new house with HARADA in curly chrome letters on the oak-type front door.

Emily too had moved. She had been acting head teacher during the headmaster's absence on war service, and was appointed head when he moved to a larger school. A little house went with the post, and as her father had died, Emily persuaded her mother to leave the cottage where she had reared her thriving family and live at Springbourne with her. Mary Clare missed her good neighbour sadly, but sometimes made the long walk over the hill to spend an hour or two with her.

Fairacre school had its changes, too. Private warnings to Mr Hope had been of no avail. The man was now a physical wreck and the work of the school suffered badly.

One spring morning he came into Dolly's room looking vaguely bewildered.

'I'm leaving Fairacre,' he said abruptly. 'I had my notice this morning.'

Dolly was not surprised, but she was sorry that he was going. There were many things about the man that she liked, and change was always distasteful to her.

'The managers suggest that I have a holiday for a month or two,' went on the headmaster, 'and there will probably be a vacancy for me in Leicestershire.'

Dolly guessed that this opening must have been suggested by Miss Parr, one of the managers of Fairacre school, who had relatives in Leicester. Privately, Dolly thought Mr Hope was lucky to get anything. She suspected that he would have an assistant's post in the new school, and in this she was right.

He left at the end of May, and Dolly wondered who would be the next occupant of the school house. Fairacre school was very much bigger than Springbourne so that a man would be appointed. For the last few weeks of term Dolly and a woman supply teacher from Caxley coped with the school between them, and in September Mr Benson arrived.

The first thing that Fairacre noticed about the new headmaster was that he had a car and a wireless set. The car was a Ford T model with a beautiful brass radiator and brass headlamps, and the wireless set was the latest type with a superior gadget to hold the cat's whisker above the crystal.

'Go ahead sort of fellow,' commented Mr Willet to Dolly Clare. Young Mr Willet had been badly wounded during the war, and was making a modest living as caretaker to the school and by growing vegetables and plants for sale in his own flourishing garden. He was clearly impressed by the new man, and so were all the other males from six to sixty, Dolly observed, for such is the power of things mechanical.

He had other interests besides the car and the wireless set. He had served with distinction in the RNAS and had travelled widely. In the few years he was at Fairacre he reminded Dolly of Mr Hope in his younger days, for he had the power to fire his listeners with his own enthusiasm. He was a great supporter of the League of Nations, and tried to explain its world-wide task to the children who only knew the small world of Fairacre.

'There will never be another war,' he promised them, many and many a time. 'This war was the war to end all wars. Now we shall use reason to settle arguments between nations.'

He bought many magazines and papers for the children from his own meagre salary. He found that they read these far more easily than books. Arthur Mee's monthly *My Magazine* was a great favourite, and Dolly remembered the frontispiece to one of the issues very clearly. It showed a little girl, barefoot and in a pink tunic, opening the golden gates to a new world where all was peace. It was typical of the ardent hope of a war-shattered world. 'Never again!' was the cry, uttered in all sincerity.

The new world certainly seemed a happy place in the years that followed. Fairacre did not boast any bright young things of its own, but its inhabitants were pleasurably shocked to read about those who painted the big cities red. *The Caxley Chronicle* reported the dancing of the Charleston at the Civic Ball in the Corn Exchange, and some of the older generation felt that the age of decadence had arrived.

There was certainly an air of gaiety about which reached even to such leafy retreats as Beech Green and Fairacre. It was a daily wonder to wake to a world at peace, to know that one's menfolk were home again, that the guns thundered no more, and that life could be relished for the good thing it was.

An enterprising firm in Caxley started a bus service during the twenties and this made a world of difference to those living in remote villages. Twice a week, on Thursday and Saturday, it was possible to ride from Fairacre through Beech Green to Caxley by bus, and there to shop or meet one's friends, or even catch another bus to the giddy pleasures of the county town fifteen miles away. The older people, whose cycling and walking days were over, were enraptured by this new wonder, and Mary Clare became a regular passenger on Thursday mornings.

'Proper old gad-about you're getting these days!' teased Francis, but he was glad to see Mary with this new interest. Now she could go to see Ada and the children much more often, and though she sometimes wondered if she were a nuisance to her daughter, the rapturous welcome she received from her two grandchildren consoled her. It was true that Ada looked with mixed feelings upon the small shabby figure, in her old-fashioned button boots and jet-trimmed bonnet, which ambled up the gravel path, always, it seemed, when she had a party of genteel Caxley friends whom she was trying to impress.

Emily and Dolly found the Saturday morning buses very useful too. They frequently met in Caxley to shop and exchange news over coffee. Edgar was never mentioned, but Dolly knew that the marriage was successful and that he had two small children. How Emily felt about it she could only guess. They were both in their thirties now, and often spoke good-humouredly of 'being on the shelf'. Chances of marriage were very small, they knew, for their generation, and Dolly counted herself lucky in having Ada's children in the family and all the young fry of Fairacre to work among. Nevertheless, her sense of loss was great, for other people's children are a very poor substitute for one's own, and there were occasions when, at that sad time of day between sunset and twilight, Dolly could not bear to think of the long lonely years ahead.

It was during Mr Benson's period of headship that Mrs Pringle was engaged as school cleaner. This dour individual, who was 'never so happy as when she was miserable', as the villagers said, had lived in Fairacre since her marriage and worked for Mrs Hope at the school house. The shortcomings of Mr Hope and the decline of his wife had furnished Mrs Pringle with ghoulish interest. She had wanted to take over the school cleaning for several years, for the two great black tortoise stoves which warmed the building exercised a strong fascination over her, and she longed to apply blacklead and elbow grease to their neglected surfaces.

'Fair makes my blood boil to see the state that Alice got 'em in,' she grumbled to Dolly on her first day in office. Alice was the poor toothless old crone who had been taken from an orphanage at ten, set to work as kitchen maid for fifty years, first here, then there, until she drifted to a hovel in Fairacre and earned a few shillings by scrubbing the school floors and lighting the stoves. In all the years that Dolly had known her she had only heard her speak about a dozen times. She bobbed and nodded when addressed, a skinny hand fluttering to her mouth.

She had been found dead in her little broken cottage, rolled up in a thin grey blanket before an empty grate, a week or two earlier, and the neighbour who had lifted her said that she was lighter than his own two-year-old.

Mrs Pringle would have made six of her. A squat, square figure clad in a thick skirt and jumper covered with a vivid flowered overall, she stumped morosely about the premises grumbling at the mess made by the children and the amount of coke consumed by the stoves. She was to be part and parcel of the Fairacre scene for many years and Dolly Clare found it best to turn a deaf ear to most of the lady's complaints.

As time passed Dolly sometimes thought that she knew every stick and stone of Fairacre school. The grain of her desk lid, the knots in the wooden partition, the clang of the door-scraper and the sound of the school bell above her were as familiar to her as her own face and voice. Only the children changed, and now she taught many whose parents had once sat in the same desks. Miss Clare was becoming an institution. Would she ever leave, she asked herself?

Mr Benson left after five years, his successor left after seven, but Miss Clare remained at her post.

'She won't never go,' the parents said to each other. 'And a good thing too. Taught us all right, she did, and teaches our kids good manners, as well as sums and reading.'

She was looked upon with affection and with much respect. The years added dignity and authority to Dolly's upright figure. Her fair hair was beginning to grey a little, but her blue eyes were as bright and kindly as ever.

'Pity she never married,' she overheard her headmaster say. 'A bit late now, I suppose,' he added and Dolly echoed the sentiment.

It was not only age, but circumstances that kept Dolly at Fairacre. In the early thirties Francis collapsed one day, while he was digging in the garden. Doctor Martin surveyed him gravely. Mary and Dolly watched the doctor closely from the other side of the bed. He was an old friend, but they rarely needed to call him in professionally. This was an alarming moment.

'I'll call again in the morning,' he said at last, leaving Francis in a heavy sleep.

The next morning he was moved to Caxley hospital, and

Mary was inconsolable. Dolly was obliged to have the week away from school to comfort her mother. They went daily to visit Francis, who lay very quiet and still, but smiled at them and occasionally spoke. He seemed very weak, and from Doctor Martin's manner Dolly guessed that this was her father's last illness.

One May evening she went alone, cycling along the scented lane. It had changed little since the first time she had driven along it behind Bella's massive bulk, but sometimes a car passed her now, where there was none before, and the main street of Caxley had more cars and lorries than horse-drawn vehicles these days. Her dislike of Caxley had changed over the years to affection. So much had happened to her there that it now seemed as much a background to her life as Beech Green and Fairacre.

Later, sitting beside her father's bed, holding his hand in hers peacefully, the feeling that she was part of Caxley stole upon her. How many other people had sat as she did now, or lay as her father did, gazing upon the trees outside that sheltered the nearby almshouses? Caxley was the mother town to which all the surrounding villages turned. Here they came to work, or sent their children to school. Here they gathered when war broke out, or a queen died, or peace was celebrated. Here were the offices which dealt with rents and rates and other irksome matters which concerned them. And here was the hospital which took them into its shelter and restored them to health, or eased their going when life ebbed.

When she left her father that evening she made her way down a quiet by-road leading from the back of the hospital to the centre of the town. She felt curiously at peace, still sustained by the feeling of being at home in the town. A motor hearse overtook her and waited to slip into the main road ahead, leading to the market place. Four men, in sober clothes, sat beside the coffin on its way to the town undertakers. There was a decent restraint about their quiet bearing which Dolly admired. A right and proper way, she thought, to make one's last journey through familiar streets, flanked by companions, slipping along unobtrusively with schoolboys on bicycles and vegetable vans, as unremarked as any other part of the moving stream. If that was what fate had in store for Francis then she felt she could face it all the more bravely from having seen the passing of that unknown one who had walked the ways of Caxley as her father had done.

He died that same night and was buried three days later beneath a giant yew tree in Beech Green churchyard not far from little Frank. Mary was braver than Dolly had dared to hope. She went to stay for a few days with Ada, and the children's chatter and affection seemed to comfort her.

When she returned she seemed her old self. She sighed with relief at being back again, lonely though it was without the dear presence of Francis.

'Ada's is lovely,' she said to Dolly. 'Full of fine things, and hot water straight from the tap and that – but it don't seem homely to me. I'm happier here.'

Later that evening she looked across the table at Dolly, who sat sewing a shirt for John Francis.

'When you was born,' she said slowly, 'the old dame that was helping said you'd be a lucky child. She said: "That child be blessed and the day will come when you'll remember what I told you." Those were her very words, Dolly, and they've come true. You've been a real blessing to me – all my days.'

Dolly was deeply moved. Her mother rarely showed emotion, and when, soon after, she kissed her goodnight, she felt that they had never before been quite so close.

Francis left very little. Almost all his money had gone to the buying of the cottage, but his thatching tools and those of his father were carefully stored in the garden shed. It was Emily who discovered a young man in Springbourne who wanted to take up a thatcher's craft, and to him Dolly and Mary gave the tools. He was a handsome lad, with a look of Frank about him, and it gave both women much happiness to think of Francis's tools being used again, on the same familiar roofs, by one of the next generation.

CHAPTER 19

LOOKING back upon those twenty years between the wars Miss Clare realised how great a change had taken place in the lives of her neighbours.

Very few of her mother's generation had been to London, or had seen the sea, although both were within seventy miles of the village. She herself had not seen either until she was in her twenties. But with more and more cars pouring into the roads, and with buses and charabancs increasing their services weekly, there were very few children in Miss Clare's class of babies who had not seen both before they were five or six years of age.

It made life much more wonderful and exciting. When you have been bounded by the limits of your legs, or bicycle wheels, there is something deeply thrilling about boarding a coach which will take you a hundred miles away. Dolly Clare never completely lost her sense of wonder at the miracle of modern speed. Holidays away from home were not possible on her small salary, but occasionally she took her mother on a day's outing to the coast, during the school vacations, and this was a rare joy for them both.

The children's annual outing was equally exciting. When Dolly was at Fairacre school as a pupil, and in her early teaching years, a brake pulled by four horses had taken them all to Sir Edmund Hurley's park just beyond Springbourne, and there, five miles from home, they had felt that they were in a foreign land.

Another new joy was the occasional visit to the theatre at the county town. To be sure, the scenery was sometimes a little shabby and some of the acting mediocre, but to Dolly and her unsophisticated friends it was always an evening of enchantment.

Even more miraculous was the wireless. In its early days, soon after Mr Benson's coming to Fairacre, the children besieged Dolly's desk each morning to tell her what the invisible uncles and aunts in Children's Hour had told them the day before. And when, one unforgettable day, they heard 'Hello, twins!' boomed forth in unison, for a pair who lived at Beech Green, their excitement knew no bounds. Sometimes, Dolly thought wryly, they seemed to learn far more from the wireless than they did from her. Would lessons ever be broadcast to the schools, she wondered?

In the little cottage in the evenings Dolly listened to concerts and satisfied that love of music which had first been fired by Arnold's wheezy phonograph. Mary's pleasure in it increased as the years went by, for her eyes soon tired of reading and sewing, and she found this new invention fascinating. There was no doubt about it, she told Dolly, life was richer by far than when she was a girl at the farm, creeping to her attic bedroom, lamp in hand, soon after darkness fell.

But despite the new wireless sets in cottage homes, and the new excitement of modern travel, things were still difficult for those employed in agriculture. Many of the children who clamoured round Dolly's desk, eagerly trying to tell her of last night's wireless programme, were thin from lack of proper food. The lot of the farmer, and, worse still, of the farm labourer, was as hard as it had ever been, and Dolly often wondered how long the land could support a fast-growing population. It was not enough to expect industry to pay for the foreign food that packed the little village shop at Beech Green and the rest of the shops in England. The farmer must be given hope and help to be able to contribute his share. It grieved Dolly to see the heritage of the countryside, held in trust for generations to come, being so sadly neglected.

For women a new interest sprang up during these years. The Women's Institute had a thriving membership at Beech Green and at Fairacre. Mary Clare was a keen supporter and acquired many new skills. Dolly was amused to see her proficiency at upholstery, and acted as unskilled assistant when her mother boldly re-stuffed and covered the ancient sofa and matching armchair. It was Dolly's job to pull the tough strings which drew the buttons into their allotted dimples, and very hard work she found it. But Mary seemed inspired by her new ability and from upholstery she progressed to making loose covers, going from strength to strength.

The years passed tranquilly. The spring term, bedecked with primroses and violets and loud with cuckoo song outside the school, and the remains of winter coughs inside, gave way to the pinks and roses of the summer term, arrayed in 'Virol' jars along the window-sills. Hips and haws and trailing bryony welcomed the autumn in, and new babies faced Miss Clare for the first time in their young lives. And always the highlights of the year remained the same – Christmas, Easter, Harvest Festival and the school outing and the church fête, held, as always, in the grounds of the vicarage.

To some women this familiar cycle would have proved stultifying. Dolly Clare saw nothing monotonous in it. She liked order, she liked knowing the pattern ahead. Within the framework of seasons' and terms' events she found variety and excitement enough. For one thing, no child was like its neighbour. More fascinating still to the elderly teacher, no child was exactly like its parents. There was something infinitely satisfying in comparing the generations of the families she knew so well. There were hereditary tendencies in looks or behaviour which were interesting to study. She knew too the background of the homes from which they came, which child went to bed too late, and which was frightened of its father and for what reason. She knew which child was jealous of a newly born brother, which one pined for one, which one resented being the youngest. There was nothing hidden from Miss Clare, as both children and parents knew, and better still, she could be trusted to keep confidences to herself. In a village a silent tongue is rare, and much respected. Dolly Clare heard many secrets, gave advice when it was asked of her, and found the study of character endlessly absorbing. Life in Fairacre, she discovered, grew richer every year, and the slow measure that she trod there pleased her more than the giddy whirling of the world outside.

The news from abroad, during the mid-thirties, was disturbing to say the least of it. The domination of Austria by the Germans, and Ethiopia by the Italians were ugly reminders to Dolly Clare of the happenings of twenty years before. Surely such appalling things could not happen again in a lifetime? She pondered on the spirit of hope which had transfigured the world at the end of the first war. Surely the League of Nations could not fail? – it had the support of all right-thinking men and women. It seemed stupid to worry over the childish posturings of Hitler and Mussolini when one considered the forces ranged against them.

So Dolly tried to comfort herself, but she was not completely successful. There was something terrifyingly insane about the

statements made by the
two dictators and Dolly
trembled to think what
might happen if they
were allowed the time
to gain further military
strength. Arrogance
unchecked becomes
megalomania, and it is
impossible to reason
with a madman. Would
the dearly-bought
peace be shattered yet
again?

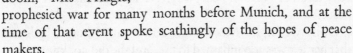

That harbinger of
doom, Mrs Pringle,
prophesied war for many months before Munich, and at the
time of that event spoke scathingly of the hopes of peace
makers.

Dolly came across her before school one morning early in
the autumn term of 1938. She was spreading newspaper round
the newly whitened stone at the base of the stove in the
infants' room. Crouched on all fours, in an unlovely toad-like
position, she stabbed vehemently with a podgy forefinger at a
photograph of Mr Chamberlain waving a piece of paper.

"Opeless!' announced Mrs Pringle. 'Just 'opeless, trying to
deal with that Hitler fellow. My mother, God rest her, would
have called this a sop to Cerebos. Mark my words, Miss Clare,
we'll 'ave to pay for this all right!'

All through that uneasy year, when a nation's conscience
grew more and more troubled as one German coup followed
another, Mrs Pringle's dire prognostications were cast like
black pearls before the surfeited swine. The headmaster at that

time, Mr Fortescue, goaded beyond endurance one hot day in the summer of 1939, sharply told her to hold her tongue.

Dolly, washing a child's sticky hands in the lobby, heard the swift intake of Mrs Pringle's outraged breath. Then the floorboards resounded to the limping gait of Mrs Pringle's substantial frame. It was obvious that her leg, always combustible in times of affront, had 'flared-up' with unusual ferocity. She stumped through the lobby, looking neither to right nor left, mouth compressed and nostrils flaring.

Dolly put her head round the classroom door. Mr Fortescue was alone, scribbling a fierce note to a dilatory publisher who had failed to send some promised inspection copies.

'We shan't see Mrs Pringle again this term, I suspect,' she said.

'That'll suit me,' replied the headmaster grimly. 'It's only another fortnight anyway. At last we shall have some peace.'

Dolly was right. Mrs Pringle sent a stilted note which said that her leg was too inflamed to use, and she did not know when she would be back.

'That means,' said Dolly, construing the letter to her colleague, who had not the same experience of Mrs Pringle's warfare, 'that we must woo her back if we want the school scrubbed out during the holidays.'

'Oh, hang it!' expostulated Mr. Fortescue. 'What an old vixen she is!' He looked doubtfully at Dolly.

'Yes, I'll go,' she offered, reading his thoughts, and on the last day of term she made a treaty with the enemy.

'It's only because his lordship's going away,' announced Mrs Pringle. 'Wild horses wouldn't drag me back inside that school if he was going to be prying about. You can tell him from me, Miss Clare, I'm coming to oblige you and because I knows my duty to the children!'

Dolly promised to deliver the message, wondering privately why Mrs Pringle's strong sense of duty to the children had remained quiescent for the past fortnight.

And so this petty storm, just one of many made by Mrs Pringle, passed over, while the storm that was to darken the whole world swept closer and closer.

At the end of August, a few days before Fairacre school, freshly scrubbed and polished, was due to reopen, the evacuation of children from London began, and Caxley and the villages around it awaited the newcomers.

Dolly and Emily went to Caxley station to help. As the long trains drew in to the platform, with heads and arms sprouting from the windows, Dolly remembered that other war, so tragically near, it seemed, when she had watched her own generation on its way to annihilation. Now these younger casualties of a new war, emerged into the shimmering heat, pale faced and heavy-eyed, clutching one another's hands and weighed down with gas masks and cases.

All through the long hot day Emily and Dolly helped to sort out the children, and returned to their own cottages with two apiece. Dolly had chosen two small sisters, June and Dawn Milligan, both tearful and bewildered. Emily, as bold as ever, had returned to Springbourne with a pair of black-haired twin boys of twelve who looked as tough and unmannerly as any among the hundreds who arrived. Dolly had no doubt that Emily would win any future battles. Her own family background and many years of teaching had given Emily a rare resilience.

On the next Sunday the Prime Minister was to speak to the nation. War looked inevitable, and Dolly and her mother sat down with heavy hearts to listen to the broadcast. The cottage door was propped open. Outside, the two little girls dressed and undressed the dolls they had brought with them, and the ghostly Emily that Dolly had unearthed from the trunk in the loft. She was sadly shabby and her stuffing had shifted so that her figure was badly deformed, but the Milligan children took her to their hearts, and Dolly was glad to see poor Emily beloved once more.

The sunshine bathed the children playing by the door, and warmed the brick floor by Mary Clare's feet. The scent of tobacco plant stole into the room as they listened to Mr Chamberlain's voice. At last it came to an end. Mary and Dolly looked silently at each other, both fearful of breaking down before the unheeding children.

At that moment, the distant wailing of Caxley's air-raid sirens began to be heard, and close at hand the banshee clamour of Beech Green's began too. The two children looked up at the cloudless sky with such pathetic terror in their faces, as they clutched their dolls to them, that Dolly's own fears were transformed to fury. It was insupportable that innocent children should have to suffer in this way – torn from their homes, set down among strangers and then forced to live in constant fear! Brave with the wrath that burned within her, she brought the two little girls indoors and calmed them, and when at last they were busy in the kitchen and the all-clear had sounded, Dolly's anger cooled.

In the last war, she thought, she had seen many men go into battle. This time the battle came to them – to all of them, women and children too. Everyone would be taking part in this war, Dolly suddenly realised, and with this thought fear was inconsequently replaced by infinite relief. Somehow, it was comforting to be in it with the men this time.

Dolly had never known anything like the term that began so soon after. A London school shared the building, and overflowed into the modest village hall nearby, a building which had been put up in memory of the Fairacre men who had died in the 1914-18 war.

Fairacre school had never been so tightly jammed. Half a dozen long desks, which had not been in use since Dolly was a child there in Edwardian days, were pulled from their resting place in the playground, scrubbed and polished, and put back into use. Kitchen chairs were set by collapsible card tables, the nature table was stripped and furnished accommodation for six more children, and every inch of space, it seemed, was occupied by the children. At first, the teachers had wondered if it would be better to let the London children and their teachers take over the building in the mornings, and the Fairacre children in the afternoon, but this presented many difficulties. Thus for the first few weeks of the war, Dolly Clare shared her room with two teachers from London, twenty of their pupils, and her own normal class.

It did not last long. The weeks slid by with no expected air raids, and the children gradually drifted back to town, followed eventually by their thankful teachers. Fairacre was left with a mere sprinkling of visitors, the Milligan children among them much to Dolly's delight, and the year slipped away with very little incident.

It was a good thing that there had been this rehearsal, for when, in September 1940, the onslaught began in earnest, the children came flocking back, and this time they stayed. No bombs fell in Fairacre throughout the war, but two were dropped at Beech Green one clear night in 1942, and Mrs Pringle knew why.

'It's the solemn truth,' said that lady, folding her arms majestically across her cardigan. 'As sure as you're standing there, Miss Clare, it was Ted Prince's bakehouse as led them Germans to Beech Green.'

Dolly began to protest, but was overborne. Mrs Pringle, in spate, swept everything before her with awful might.

'He says 'isself as 'e opened up the oven to see if it was all right for the loaves. Twenty to five that was. *Twenty to five!*' repeated Mrs Pringle thrusting her face belligerently towards Dolly. 'And what 'appens?'

'I don't know,' admitted Dolly weakly.

'I'll tell you. Up goes the glare from Ted's oven! Down comes the bombs at *exactly nineteen minutes to five!* That's the answer. And lucky Ted Prince might think 'isself to have no innocent deaths laid at 'is door!'

She stumped away before her argument could be taken up, and the children who had been listening enthralled to this exposition stored up the pleasurable story of Ted Prince's villainy for future telling.

Mary Clare had been in bad health for the whole of that winter, and early in 1943 Dolly sent for Doctor Martin, despite her mother's protests. Mary was in bed with a severe cough and a temperature, and Doctor Martin closed the door of the box staircase carefully when he returned from visiting the patient.

'Sit down, Dolly,' he said. They faced each other across the table, Dolly more frightened than she cared to admit.

'Can you stay at home, do you think? Or get someone in?' he asked. 'What about Ada?'

Dolly thought quickly. She hated the idea of leaving her teaching, but her mother would never tolerate Ada about her if she were ill. There was no one that she could ask. Everyone in war time was busy.

'I think I could manage it,' she answered as calmly as she could.

'Good girl,' said the doctor, patting her hand kindly. 'If you keep her warm and on a light diet, she should be up and about again in a month or so.'

'A month?' cried Dolly. 'Is she as ill as that?'

'She'll probably see us both out,' answered Doctor Martin heartily, 'but she wants cosseting through the winter. Now, don't worry yourself too much. See if the school can run without you, and settle here with your mother and have a rest yourself.'

And so Dolly made her plans and nursed her mother for a month. Mary was an unusually good patient, delighted to see friends and fonder of her wireless set than ever. But to Dolly's anxious eyes she did not look robust, and her appetite grew smaller and smaller.

"Tis sticking in this old bed,' said Mary cheerfully one spring evening. 'Now it's getting warmer I'll sit outside in the garden and the fresh air will soon put me right.'

Dolly lifted the untouched supper tray and went towards the door.

'Bring your sewing up here tonight,' said Mary. 'I reckon that old dame knew a thing or two when she said you'd be a blessing to me. How would I have got on without you this winter?'

'Ada would have had you,' answered Dolly reasonably.

'She ain't worth the half of you,' said the old lady dispassionately, 'and never was – for all Francis thought of her!'

Dolly laughed, but could not help a warm glow at the sincerity of her mother's remark. She returned with her sewing, and they talked for an hour or so, until Mary yawned and settled down for the night.

In the morning Dolly carried up a cup of tea, to find her mother in exactly the same position, with her hands clasped lightly upon the white bedspread and a look of utter contentment upon her face. But the room was uncannily still, and when Dolly touched her mother's enlaced hands, they were cold in death.

CHAPTER 20

D OLLY was glad to return to her crowded classroom a week after her mother's death. The cottage seemed bleak without her warm presence, and Dolly was grateful for the return of the Milligan children. A neighbour had offered to put them up on the day of Mary's death, and they stayed there until after the funeral. Dolly had found her week of solitude profoundly depressing. Worn out with nursing, deprived now of both parents whom she had loved dearly, and low in health through meagre war-time diet, Dolly wondered if she were really fit to take charge of children again. All her instincts were to return to the cheering bustle of the school-room, but such weariness possessed her that she doubted if she could ever teach again.

She need not have feared. The comfort of the children's presence at school and the Milligans' at home did much to restore her spirits, though she often longed to have another grown-up with her in the evenings when the little girls had been put to bed.

Emily came over sometimes, but was tied with her own two evacuees and her ageing mother.

'One day we'll share a house,' Emily promised. 'And I'll give you your breakfast in bed one day and you shall do it for me the next!'

'Then it shall be in this house,' Dolly said, 'and you can choose your own bedroom – the one with the sparrows or the one with the house-martins outside.'

And so, half in jest, they made their plans for the future, though each wondered secretly if circumstances would ever allow them the pleasure of sharing a home. It seemed as if the war would never end. The drone of bombers in the night sky, as they set off from an airfield to the west of Caxley, was the noise to which the inhabitants of that area fell asleep. There was a dour, business-like approach to this war, Dolly thought, quite different from the tragically idealistic outlook of the earlier one. It was a job to be done, as efficiently and as ruthlessly as possible, and though the young men possessed the same courage and endurance as their fathers, no poets sang them into battle. Dolly's generation had lived through a war to end war, followed by a period of hopes and dreams. There could be no glamour about this conflict which shattered the illusions of a quarter of a century.

Ada's son, John Francis, was a bomber pilot, and Dolly shared his parents' anxiety for him. He was stationed in Yorkshire, and occasionally Ada made the tedious journey northward to see him, staying at the local inn with other wives and mothers. Dolly marvelled at her bravery throughout the war years. Her robust good health and spirits seemed to thrive in adversity, and she never showed her fears before her friends. She had volunteered for driving with the R.A.F. at the beginning of the war, and spent a large part of her time on the road.

The terms dragged by. After D-Day, in June 1944, some of the London children returned to town, as the war seemed to be nearing its end, but the Milligan children remained at Beech Green. Dolly wondered how she would feel when they too returned. She hoped they would stay for a long time.

At last, in May 1945, the long-awaited European peace came. Dolly's thoughts turned back to that earlier war as she listened to the joyous pealing of bells across the spring meadows around her. This time she mourned no lover. Her nephew, John Francis, remained unscathed, though many of his friends had gone, and Dolly was thankful for this mercy.

In the months that followed, while the world waited for fighting to end in the Pacific and the Far East, Dolly wondered what the future held. This war was not ending with the same firm conviction of an ever-lasting peace, as when the first world war came to an end. On the contrary, it seemed almost as if the thought of future wars was present in people's minds. Mr Willett voiced many people's feelings when he spoke to Dolly one morning.

'Got them Germans beat for a second time,' he announced cheerfully, 'and now I s'pose it's them Russians next.'

'But, Mr Willett,' protested Dolly, 'they're our allies!'

'Hmph!' snorted the caretaker disbelievingly, 'how long for, I'd like to know? Best by far polish 'em off while we're at it!'

It was not long after this conversation that the horror of Hiroshima's bombing burst upon the world. The frightening possibilities of warfare in the future clouded the rejoicing which accompanied the final stage of the war. Now, it seemed, not what kind of a world would we live in, but would there be a world at all, as mankind had always known it? Sitting before her innocent babes that summer, Dolly Clare wondered what hopes she could put before them. It had been much simpler at the end of the first world war. Then she and Mr Hope had honestly believed that the world would be built anew upon the ashes of the old, and that the sacrifice of thousands of young lives had not been in vain. They had been able to speak with conviction and hope to the children before them. But now those same children had experienced a war themselves, and many had made the same sacrifice. What could she say to their children now?

She could only pass on to them the philosophy which sustained her throughout her life. She could teach them to face whatever came with calmness and courage, to love their families and their friends with unswerving loyalty, and to relish the lovely face of the countryside in which they lived. It might seem a humdrum, day-to-day set of values, but Dolly

Clare knew from long experience that they could carry a man bravely through a lifetime's vicissitudes.

In 1944 an Act of Parliament was passed which had an important effect upon the lives of Dolly Clare and those like her. This Education Act meant that almost all the older children in the villages around Caxley would leave the small schools after eleven years of age and be taught together in one of three types of secondary school, grammar, technical, or modern. Furthermore, the school leaving age was raised to fifteen, and this meant an extra year at school.

It was impossible to put this revolutionary idea into practice immediately. Beech Green school was to have a large extension to take the over-elevens from the small schools nearby, including those from Fairacre and Springbourne, and was to be called 'Beech Green Secondary Modern School'. Children who were assessed as intelligent enough to profit by a grammar school education would go to the ancient Caxley Grammar School, as had been the custom for generations. Those who seemed best fitted for a technical school were destined to share the secondary modern schools' amenities, for no technical school was to materialise for many years.

The effect of this step was far-reaching. The children themselves much resented the extra year, Dolly found. Country children have traditionally been early wage earners, and those who were looking forward to leaving Mr Fortescue's care and launching out on their own in a year or two's time felt thwarted when they found that they must mark time for another twelve-month. For, despite the high-flown theories about the advantages of a further year's schooling, the truth of the matter was that there were very few schools equipped, either in apparatus or staff, to make the extra time of any real value to the last-year pupils. In time this would be altered, but immediately after the war, labour and materials were short, money was needed desperately for other aspects of national recovery, and the schools struggled to put into practice a project which was almost unworkable in the circumstances. Nevertheless, Dolly and her fellow teachers realised that it was indeed a step forward which should, in time, prove a wise move.

Another result of the Act was the transfer of some church schools to the County Education Committee, for the managers had to undertake to bear half the cost of improvements and maintenance. Springbourne was one of these schools. Fairacre's managers decided to continue as a church school, and undertook to find the money for its upkeep.

During the next year or two Dolly found teaching a difficult task. Mr Fortescue was due to retire in 1949. He was certainly ready for it. To Dolly's eyes, he looked twenty years older than he had at the outbreak of war, and the addition of a dozen or so resentful fourteen-year-olds to his normal class taxed him sorely. He did his best to contrive useful work of a more advanced nature for them, but without equipment he could not undertake carpentry, metalwork or the electrical work which they would have enjoyed and profited from learning. He organised an occasional trip to Caxley to watch a council meeting or to visit factories there, but the children sensed that it was all a makeshift passing-of-time, and longed to be in a job where they could be earning money, as their older brothers and sisters had done at the same age.

Dolly was now approaching sixty, and though she was as upright as ever, her hair was snow white and she suffered from occasional twinges of rheumatism. She still cycled daily the three miles from Beech Green to Fairacre, and still looked out with fresh joy for the coming of each year's violets and wild roses along that well-loved route. During the war school dinners had come, to stay for ever it appeared, and this extra duty taxed Dolly's strength more than she realised.

Twice, during the last few years of Mr Fortescue's rule, Dolly suffered a momentary black-out, all the more alarming because she had no warning of the sudden attack. On both occasions she was in her own classroom, the children appeared to notice nothing, and she did not mention either occurrence to her headmaster, dismissing the incidents as the result of being rather over-tired, as indeed she was.

Life alone at the cottage was very quiet without June and Dawn. Dolly had grown accustomed to their chatter and the pounding of their young feet overhead in the little bedroom. She had always prepared an evening meal while they were there, but now that she was alone she could not be bothered to cook, after a day's teaching, and took a glass of milk and a biscuit to an early bed. She hated to think of the empty room next door where first she and Amy and then the two Milligan children had slept. She herself now slept in the room which had been her parents', and very lonely she found it as autumn gave way to the cold of winter.

One windy January evening Emily came to see her. They sat by the fire and Emily told Dolly some surprising news. Springbourne school was to be closed as its numbers had fallen steadily and it now boasted only sixteen pupils.

'And what about you?' asked Dolly.

'I'm to be transferred to a school in Caxley. That dreadful old place by the gasworks that's now called "Hillside Secondary Modern School". Not much modern about that ancient monument,' said Emily, poking the fire vigorously.

'But where will you live?' persisted Dolly. The thought of Emily leaving the nearby village was shocking.

'With Joe,' said Emily. 'It all works out very well. His housekeeper gave up at Christmas and he's glad to put me up in exchange for looking after things. I shall enjoy it.'

Dolly said nothing, but she wondered if Emily really would enjoy it. Her mother had died a few months earlier so that she was free to go to Joe, but the two had never got on very well. He was the youngest of the Davis brood, and a bachelor of about fifty years of age. By trade he was a plumber, and, by the Davis's standards, a well-to-do man. Natural shyness had kept him from marriage, though it was well-known in the family that a personable widow in the same Caxley road pursued him relentlessly. So far he had resisted her enticements.

'You must come into Caxley and see me often,' continued Emily, busy with the poker. 'Joe was always fond of you.'

It would not be quite the same, Dolly felt, to visit Emily in someone else's home, but she promised to go frequently, and begged Emily to spend as much time as she could at Beech Green. She looked at her friend in the firelight. Her hair was sprinkled with silver threads but was still, in the main, the crisp dark crop she had known since they were children. Emily had altered little over the years, and still had the power to give that same comfort to Dolly as the first unforgettable Emily had done in her infant years. This was a sad moment for them both. Life in a Caxley street, no matter how comfortable Joe's home was, could not be as happy for Emily as her own rural independence.

'When must you go?' asked Dolly, at last.

'I start there next term,' said Emily. 'I shall move in the Easter holidays.'

She looked at the clock upon the mantelshelf and uttered a cry of horror.

'So late! Never mind, I've only myself to think of,' she said, putting on her coat. 'When I'm a housekeeper I shall have to take more care!'

Dolly walked to the gate with her through the windy night. The light of Emily's bicycle wavered along the brick path, and the moon emerged from scudding clouds for a brief moment. By its gleam Dolly caught sight of Emily's face. It was sad, but had the dogged look about it with which she had always faced misfortune.

She watched her old friend mount her bicycle, called farewell, and watched the brave little light until a bend of the road extinguished it. Dolly went to bed that night with a heavy heart.

It was a relief to everybody when Beech Green's new buildings were ready and the long-awaited transfer of the older children took place. Fairacre's parents had been vociferous about the scandal of moving their offspring at first. Later, they said it was 'a crying shame they never learnt nothing in their last year' at Fairacre, and it was high time they went on to Beech Green's superior instruction at eleven.

Mr Fortescue had just retired, and as Fairacre was now a primary school only, a woman head was appointed. Dolly Clare liked Miss Read from the first, and the two worked well together. It was much more peaceful with the bigger children absent. Playground duty was far less arduous, and fewer numbers in the classroom meant that it was easier to give the children individual help in a quiet atmosphere.

Dolly was grateful for a less busy working day. She had been obliged to go to Doctor Martin's surgery one day and confess that she had had 'a turn'. The old doctor listened gravely to her heart and shook his head.

'Feel like retiring?' he asked.

'No,' said Miss Clare composedly.

'I thought not,' replied the doctor. He surveyed his old friend with a gleam of amusement. 'Well, take one of these tablets once a day, and try to rest more. I suppose I might just as well talk to that table there, but that's my advice, Dolly.'

It was soon after this encounter that fate struck again. One autumn afternoon, the children were engrossed in making bunches of corn to decorate St Patrick's church next door for Harvest Festival. It was a time that Dolly always loved. She loved the clean floury smell of the grain, and the sight of the busy children preparing to garland the sombre old church. She sat at her desk watching their solemn faces as they arranged the heads of corn evenly together.

It was warm and close, and suddenly the room began to tilt alarmingly. Her heart began to beat so loudly that she felt the children must hear it. She struggled to rise from her chair to open a window, but the last thing she was conscious of was the stream of water which flowed across the desk top from an overturned vase of pink dahlias.

Later she found herself in the school house with Doctor Martin gazing steadily at her.

'I'm sorry,' she whispered.

'Nothing to be sorry about,' he replied cheerfully. 'You can't control your heart's antics, you know.'

Dolly heard his voice as he made his farewells to the head mistress. She knew suddenly, with devastating clarity, that this was the end of the life she loved at Fairacre. She was no more use to the children if these attacks were to become frequent. She must have frightened them to death by this afternoon's collapse. It was not right to stay in her condition.

The room swam before her tear-filled eyes, but her voice was steady when her headmistress came in to see her.

'I shall go at Christmas,' she said, and felt as though her heart would break.

Retirement was something which Dolly had dreaded. To be idle, to be useless, to be laid aside, seemed appalling to her. But when it actually happened, and she had made the sad farewells to the school she had known all her life, and had put a generous cheque from the managers in the bank and a presentation clock upon her bedside table, she found that there were compensations in this time of enforced leisure.

At first she looked at her new clock and thought of what they would be doing in the classroom at that time. Now they would be out in the playground, now they would be at arithmetic, now washing their hands ready for school dinner. But gradually other activities engaged her attention, and she found it wholly delightful to potter in the garden when she would have been marking a register or collecting savings money.

Emily retired very soon after, for she was a little older than Dolly, but still she kept house for Joe and the two seemed to get along very well together. Once or twice she suggested to him that he might find another housekeeper, and that Dolly could do with her company, but he seemed so distressed by the idea that she did not pursue the subject. The friendly widow called as often as ever, and played cards on two evenings a week. On these occasions Emily and Dolly usually met.

To augment a tiny pension, Dolly Clare occasionally took in a lodger. Her first was a redoubtable young woman called Hilary Jackson, who taught her own infants' class at Fairacre school. It began as a happy relationship, for Dolly looked forward to the girl's return at the end of each day, and to hearing the school news. But she soon found that Hilary Jackson's love affairs were too tempestuous to endure, and when at last the girl decided to leave the district Dolly Clare was relieved to see her go.

One or two temporary lodgers followed, but Doctor Martin decided that his patient was doing too much, and finally forbade her to take more.

'Better to have less money than too much worry,' he told her. 'See how it goes, my girl. You'll manage, I expect. Pity you and Ada don't get on better. You could share a house with her.'

'Never!' said Dolly forthrightly, thinking of HARADA in all its ostentatious glory. It now had a billiard room, two tennis courts and a swimming pool, and Ada was in the throes of choosing the third car for the establishment. Dolly felt that she could never fit into such grandeur.

Doctor Martin had been right, she discovered. She went gently on her way with only a beloved cat for company in the house. She was not lonely now, for in a village there are always people to call and be called upon, and everyone was fond of old Miss Clare. Her garden was one of the loveliest in Beech Green, and the little thatched house always as gracious and serene as its owner. The furniture might be old, but it shone like silk; the rugs might be threadbare, but they were spotless, and everywhere there were flowers from the garden to add colour and fragrance to the cottage rooms.

And always, more precious with every passing year, was the friendship of Emily.

CHAPTER 21

OLD Miss Clare stirred in the hot sunshine. While she had dozed among her memories, the June sun had slid round the sky and now fell fully upon her head. It was too much even for Miss Clare's thin blood, and she rose and made her way towards the house.

Heat shimmered across the silvery thatch, and the great pink poppies had fallen wide open in the heat. A bumble bee fumbled up and down the blue spire of a lupin, and the cat lay stretched at full length in the shade of the hedge.

Stepping down into the cool twilight of the living-room was like entering a shady wood from some bright open meadow. The clock said four and Miss Clare spread the table with a white cloth for which Mary had made the lace edging long ago.

Humming happily to herself she went gently to and fro between the kitchen and living-room as she had done ever since she was a little girl of six. Soon Emily would arrive by bus, for this was market day in Caxley and an extra bus drove the villagers back in good time for their husbands' homecoming.

She set out her best china, a dish of plum jam, a plate of wafer-thin bread and butter, and a freshly-made sponge cake. The kettle was beginning to sing as she heard the bus stop obligingly at her gate.

'Must be Bill Prince driving,' said Miss Clare aloud. He had once been a pupil of Emily's at Springbourne and would look after his old teacher well, she knew.

The two friends met in the path and kissed affectionately.

'Come inside, where it's cooler,' said Miss Clare. 'I'll make tea at once, if you like to put your bag upstairs.'

Emily paused at the foot of the box staircase, her grey eyes sparkling.

'Doll, I've got the most wonderful news for you!'

At that moment the shrill whistle of the kettle shattered the peace of the room, and Dolly Clare hastened to the kitchen.

'Tell me when you come down!' she called.

A few minutes later, with the tea cups steaming and the bread and butter on their plates, Miss Clare looked across at her friend. Emily was obviously bubbling with excitement. Her clear grey eyes were as mischievous as a kitten's.

'Joe's given in at last,' she announced. 'On Tuesday he said he'd marry Caroline.'

Miss Clare put down her cup with a crash, and stared dumfounded.

'I can't believe it!' she cried at last. 'After all these years!'

The full significance of the disclosure suddenly dawned upon her. She put a thin hand upon her friend's.

'And you're free? You can come here?' she asked, with a quiver in her voice.

Emily nodded, smiling.

'If you still want me,' she said.

'As soon as you like,' said Miss Clare thankfully. The little room seemed lit with more than sunshine. A great happiness suffused her. At last the little house would be a shared home again. The empty bedroom would be occupied, and her companion for the last years of her long life would be the dearest and most constant friend of all. There were no words to express her joy at this sudden blessing.

Later, in the evening, they sat in the quiet garden and discussed plans. The wedding was to be as soon as possible. Caroline obviously had the sense to act swiftly after years of waiting, and she and Joe proposed to live in his house as soon as they were married.

'I ought to be able to come next month,' said Emily. 'In nice time to help with the bottling and jamming.'

'And to think,' sighed Dolly happily, 'that you'll be here to enjoy it next winter! I still can't believe it's happened!'

They sat there until the white owl from the elms nearby swooped out on his nightly affairs, and the moths began to flutter in the twilight. Then the two old friends walked slowly indoors and prepared for bed.

'This has always seemed like home to me,' said Emily, when Miss Clare came to say goodnight. 'It's lovely to be in Beech Green again. I started my life here, and I hope I'll end it here, Dolly. It's funny when you think of it – the furthest I've been is Dorset, and the furthest you've been is Norfolk. I suppose some people would think our lives have been narrow, and would feel sorry for us. But I think we've been two of the luckiest women alive – to have lived all our lives in this dear small place and to have watched the children grow up and have children of their own, and always to have had our friends about us.'

'I thank God daily,' answered Dolly simply, 'for the same things.'

Half an hour later, Miss Clare, in her nightdress, leant from her window to take a final look at the sleeping garden. The scent of the tobacco plant floated from below, a bat rustled on its erratic way, and in the distance the white owl hooted over Hundred Acre field.

There was still a lightness in the sky and the splendid whale-back of the eternal downs was visible. Dolly Clare looked up to them with affection. How many thousands of men and women, she wondered, through countless centuries had lifted up their eyes to those great hills and there found help as she had done throughout her long life?

Beside her, a few feet along the roof her father had thatched so well, Emily's dormer window glowed companionably. It was good to know that through summer sunshine and winter storm they would share the same roof and the same view for the rest of their time on this earth. It might not be for long, but, no matter how long or how brief their allotted time, it would be a blessing shared.

Dolly Clare took one last look at the night's beauty and then, with a thankful heart, crept softly to bed.